Dillon knew it was rude to stare.

But he couldn't help himself. He was so amazed to be seeing *her* again after so many years. She'd literally knocked the wind out of him, and now, in typical Isabel style, she wanted to run away.

"Stay a while," he said, his gaze lingering a little too long on her face. "Stay and tell me why you were taking my picture."

"No." She tried to move away. She didn't want to be with Dillon Murdock.

But he refused to let her go. "Then stay long enough to tell me why you came back to Wildwood."

Wanting to show him he couldn't get to her the way he used to, Isabel retorted, "I think a better question would be—what are *you* doing here?"

"Well, that's real simple, Isabel," he said sarcastically. "I came back at my mother's request." Backing away, he called, "Yes, the prodigal son has returned."

Books by Lenora Worth

Love Inspired

The Wedding Quilt #12
Logan's Child #26
I'll Be Home for Christmas #44
Wedding at Wildwood #53

LENORA WORTH

grew up in a small Georgia town and decided in the fourth grade that she wanted to be a writer. But first, she married her high school sweetheart, then moved to Atlanta, Georgia. Taking care of their baby daughter at home while her husband worked at night, Lenora discovered the world of romance novels and knew that's what she wanted to write. And so she began.

A few years later, the family settled in Shreveport, Louisiana, where Lenora continued to write while working as a marketing assistant. After the birth of her second child, a boy, she decided to pursue her dream full-time. In 1993, Lenora's hard work and determination finally paid off with that first sale.

"I never gave up, and I believe my faith in God helped get me through the rough times when I doubted myself," Lenora says. "Each time I start a new book, I say a prayer, asking God to give me the strength and direction to put the words to paper. That's why I'm so thrilled to be a part of Steeple Hill's Love Inspired line, where I can combine my faith in God with my love of romance. It's the best combination."

Wedding at Wildwood
Lenora Worth

Love Inspired®

Published by Steeple Hill Books™

STEEPLE HILL BOOKS

Steeple
Hill™

ISBN 0-373-87053-1

WEDDING AT WILDWOOD

Printed in U.S.A.

It was right that we should make merry and be glad,
for your brother was dead and is alive again,
and was lost and is found.

—*Luke* 15:32

To my brothers, Windell, Waymon
and especially Jerry

And in memory of
my father,
Delma Humphries

Chapter One

She hadn't planned on coming back to Wildwood. But now that she was here, Isabel Landry realized she also hadn't planned on the surge of emotions pouring over her like a warm summer rain as she stood looking up at the stark white mansion.

Wildwood.

The house, built sometime before the Civil War, was old and run-down now. Abandoned and gloomy. And so very sad.

But then, most of her memories of growing up on this land made Isabel feel sad and forlorn, too. Staring across the brilliant field of colorful wildflowers in shades of pink, yellow and fuchsia, she clicked her camera, focusing on the old house, deliberately blurring the pink phlox, purple heather, and yellow black-eyed Susans that posed a sharp contrast to the wilted condition of the once grand mansion. Now shuttered and closed, its paint peeling and its porches overgrown with ivy and wisteria, the house with the fat

Doric columns and the wide, cool verandas on each floor didn't seem as formidable as it had so long ago.

Isabel had never lived in Wildwood, but oh, how she'd dreamed of living in just such a house one day. Now, she saw that fantasy as silly, fueled by the imagination of an only child of older parents, raised on land that did not belong to her family. Born on the Murdock land, in a quiet corner of southwest Georgia, known as Wildwood Plantation.

Glancing away from the imposing plantation house, she saw where she had lived off in the distance, around the curve of the oak trees and dogwoods lining the dirt lane. The small white-framed farmhouse hadn't changed much in the ten years since she'd been away, and neither had Isabel's determined promise to herself to rise above her poor upbringing.

"I don't belong here," she said to the summer wind. "I never did."

Yet she lifted her camera, using it as a shield as she took a quick picture of the rickety little house she remembered so well. Just therapy, she told herself. That's why she'd taken the picture; she certainly didn't need or want a reminder of her years growing up there.

Looking up to the heavens, she whispered, "Oh, Mama, why did God bring me back here? I don't want this." Silently, she wondered if her deceased parents were as at peace up there in Heaven as they'd always seemed to be when they were alive and working here on Wildwood Plantation.

Mentally chiding herself, she smiled. "I know, Mama. Grammy Martha would scold me for doubting

God's intent. You are at peace. This I know. So, why can't I find that same peace here on earth?''

Lifting up yet another prayer, Isabel knew she wouldn't find any answers here on this red Georgia clay. Ever since her grandmother, Martha Landry, had called asking her to come home to take pictures of Eli Murdock's upcoming wedding, she'd been at odds. But between assignments and with nothing pressing on her agenda, she'd had no choice but to come. Isabel knew her duties, and she was good at her job as a professional photographer. Besides, she could never turn down a request from Grammy Martha, even if it did mean having to face the Murdocks and bow to their commands once again.

She hadn't been home in a long time, and she missed her grandmother. Often in the years since her parents had died—first her mother, then two years later, her father—Isabel had hurried home for quick visits with her grandmother. But on those occasions, she'd distanced herself from the Murdocks, always staying only a couple of days, sleeping in her old room at the farmhouse and keeping a low profile. During those rare trips, she'd never once ventured up the lane to visit the people who'd allowed her grandmother to stay on their land and still employed her grandmother's services on occasion.

Now, she'd be forced to socialize with them, to snap happy pictures of Eli's wedding to a girl Isabel had graduated high school with, a woman almost ten years younger than Eli. Well, at least Susan Webster was a wonderful woman. She'd make Eli a good wife, though for the life of her, Isabel couldn't understand what had attracted petite, perky Susan to such a bully bear of a man.

"Oh, well, that's none of my concern," she reminded herself as she turned back to the mansion. She'd do her job, get her pay, then be on her way again to parts unknown. But right now, she wanted to get a shot of the house with the brilliant sunset behind it, and the wavering wildflowers out in the meadow in front of it. Then she'd head back to have supper with Grammy.

Finding a good angle, Isabel focused on the house, finding a side view so the massive columns lining the front of the two-storied house would be silhouetted in the sun's glowing rays. With a flip of her wrist, she pushed her long blond hair back over her shoulders, then lifted her camera to click.

Then her heart stopped.

Through the lens, she saw a man standing at the edge of the wildflower patch on the other side of the house. Gasping, she dropped her arms down, almost dropping her expensive camera in the process. But surprise aside, Isabel knew a good shot when she saw one. She wanted to capture the man, whoever he might be, in the picture because the expression on his dark, rugged face clearly mirrored the mood of the mansion he stood staring up at.

Watching him as if he were a wild animal, Isabel barely moved for fear he'd spot her and bolt away. He looked that untamable, that intense. So intense in fact, that he wasn't even aware she was just around the corner, hiding underneath a clump of tall camellia bushes.

For a minute, Isabel analyzed him, preparing herself for her subject. Tall, at least six feet, fit enough to fill out his faded jeans nicely, and…brooding. Definitely brooding. From the five o'clock shadow on his face and the stiff tufts of spiky hair on his forehead, he looked as if he had a chip on his broad shoulders that couldn't be knocked off. His clipped dark hair mocked the wind playing through it, and every now and then, he'd lift a hand to scissor his fingers through the clump of hair that refused to stay off his face, the action speaking much louder than any gruff words he might want to shout out. This man was angry at someone or something. And…his actions seemed so familiar, so stirring.

Isabel wanted to capture that mood on film. Her artistic instincts had never failed her before. And the way her heart was beating now was a sure sign that she was on to something big here. She might not ever sell this photo, but she had to have this picture. Right now, while the light was playing off the planes and angles of his shadowed face.

Lifting her camera, she once again focused and then, holding her breath at the sheer poignant beauty of the shot, clicked the camera—once, twice, three times.

The third time, she moved closer.

And that's when the man looked up and spotted her.

"Hey!" he shouted, a dark scowl covering his face as he began a mad stalk through the wildflowers like a raging bull about to attack. "What do you think you're doing there, lady?"

Not one to take any unnecessary chances—she'd been in far more dangerous situations, but for some strange reason this man scared her—Isabel smiled and waved. "Just taking a picture. Thanks."

Then she turned and as fast as her sandaled feet and flowing skirt could carry her, headed toward the lane, the echo of that deep, commanding voice wafting through her head on that vague mist of familiarity she'd felt on first seeing the man.

"Hey, wait a minute!"

She could *feel* him stomping after her. Picking up her pace, she trudged over delicate wildflowers, forgetting to follow the worn path that had been molded through the field over the years. Whoever he was, she'd apparently made him angry by interrupting his solitude. Maybe she should at least apologize and explain, but too many warning bells were clashing loudly in her head, telling her to get away.

"You're on private property," the man called, nearer now.

Isabel didn't dare turn around, but from all the thrashing sounds, she knew he was gaining on her. Then, telling herself this was silly and that she really should speak to the man at least, she whirled just as he reached her. And came crashing into his firm chest.

The action sent the unprepared man sprawling backward even as he reached out a hand to grab Isabel. Which meant she went sprawling down with him, her camera still in one shaky hand.

Her breath coming hard, Isabel looked down at the man holding her, the scent of sweet flowers and rich loam wafting out around them as he stared up at her, a look of surprise coloring his features as his gaze moved over her face.

When she looked down into his gray eyes, Isabel

gasped again as recognition hit her hard and fast, and a very real fear coursed through her. "Dillon?"

He squinted up at her, then as realization dawned in his deep blue-gray eyes, he dropped his hands away from her shoulders so she could get up. In a voice as hard-edged and grainy as the soil beneath them, he looked her over, his surprised gaze sweeping her face. "Isabel."

It was a statement, said on a breath of disbelief.

Fussing with her blouse and skirt, Isabel used the brief time to gather her skittish thoughts. Had she also heard a bit of longing in his voice? Refusing to acknowledge her own longing, she turned to look him square in the face. "I'm sorry, Dillon. I didn't realize who you were until you got close."

Something in her drawling, soft-spoken words made Dillon Murdock's squint deepen back into a scowl. He'd remembered that sweet voice in his dreams, in his memories, and he'd often wished he could hear it again in reality.

Maybe he was just wishing again now. The dusk was obviously playing tricks on his mind. After all, it wasn't every day a man found a beautiful woman with long waves of blond hair and eyes as green as a pine forest, standing in the middle of a field of wildflowers as if she'd been waiting just for him. The same way Isabel used to wait right here for him.

To waylay the uneven beat of his heart, he said, "Well, since *you're* the one who knocked *me* flat on my back, maybe you'd better tell me what you're doing taking pictures of Wildwood."

He didn't know why she was here, Isabel thought wistfully. But then, he had no reason to know anything about her. They hadn't exactly kept in touch over the years. And they'd both changed, obviously.

Last time she'd seen Dillon, he'd only been out of high school a few months, and in a rebellious resistance he'd sported long, scraggly hair and a thick beard. Now, the hair was different, cut short and spiky, and only the remnants of a day's worth of beard covered his brooding face. Yet, she'd sensed something so familiar in him. Too familiar.

Determination and bitterness clouding her dreams away, she rose to her feet to stare down at him. "Relax, I'm just here to take pictures of your brother's wedding."

Dillon sat still, then let out a hissing breath before he stood to follow her retreating floral cotton skirts. Isabel. The minute he'd said her name, all the memories had come rushing back. Boy, she'd certainly changed from the scrawny, dirty-faced kid with cropped blond hair and bony knees. The last time he'd seen Isabel... He wasn't ready to remember the last time he'd seen her. Not yet.

"Isabel?" he called now, refusing to go back to the dark days of his youth. "Hey, wait a minute, will you?"

"You told me I was on private property," she reminded him with a haughty toss of her long locks. "I'm late, anyway."

Stubborn as ever, Dillon thought as he hurried his booted feet after her. And more beautiful than he'd ever imagined. Little Isabel, the poor kid whose father had worked the land so hard it had eventually killed him. Little Isabel, whom Eli and he had teased unrelentingly all through grammar school and high school. Isabel, afraid and ashamed, defiant and lost, a young girl who'd worn her feelings on her sleeves and carried her heart in her hand.

He'd known the girl all his life. Now he wanted to know the woman. "Isabel," he said as he reached out to grab her arm. "I'm sorry."

She whirled to face him in the muted dusk, thinking his apologies always had come too easily. "Sorry for what? I was the one who got caught where I wasn't supposed to be. Some things never change."

He jammed a hand through his hair in frustration. "Well, you're certainly right about that." Her words only reminded him of all the things he'd done to bring his life to this point. Glancing back at the house looming in the distance, he said, "I don't know why I came back here."

"Me, either," Isabel said, some of her anger disappearing. Why should she be angry with Dillon for questioning her about being on Murdock property? She'd always been a hindrance to the powerful Murdocks, anyway. And she'd do best to remember that now, when her heart was pounding and her mind was reeling at seeing Dillon again. "I'd better get back to Grammy," she said at last, to break the intensity of his dusk gray eyes.

Dillon knew it was rude to stare, but he couldn't help himself, and besides, he'd never been one to fall back on manners. He was so amazed to be standing here, seeing her again after so many years. She'd literally knocked the wind out of him, and now in typical Isabel style, she wanted to run away. "Stay a while," he said, his hand still on her bare arm, his gaze lingering a bit too long on her face. "Stay and tell me why you were taking my picture."

"No." She tried to pull away. She did not want to be with Dillon Murdock.

But he refused to let her go. "Then stay long enough to tell me why you came back to Wildwood—and don't tell me it was just to take a few pictures."

Wanting to show him he couldn't get to her the way he used to when they were younger, Isabel retorted, "I think a better question would be—what are *you* doing back here, Dillon?"

He dropped her arm then to step back, away from the accusation and condemnation he saw in her eyes. "Well now, that's real simple, Isabel," he said in a voice silky with sarcasm. "I came back at my mother's request, to witness my brother's happy nuptials." He shrugged, then lifted a hand in farewell, or maybe dismissal. Backing away, he called, "Yes, the prodigal son has returned."

With that, he turned into the gathering twilight, his dark silhouette highlighted by the rising moon and the silvery shadow of Wildwood—the house that once had been his home.

"Dillon, wait," Isabel called a few seconds later. When he just kept walking, she hurried after him. "I'm sorry. I shouldn't question your being here. You have every right to be here."

"Do I?" he asked as he whirled around to face her, his hands thrust into the pockets of his jeans, his eyes flashing like quicksilver. "Do I really, Isabel?"

"It's still your home," she reminded him as they faced each other in front of the house. "And it's still beautiful."

Dillon snorted and inclined his head toward the other side of the country road, away from the mansion. *"That's* not my home, and that house is not beautiful. Not to me."

Isabel shifted her gaze to the big house sitting across the way. Eli's modern new luxury home. Grammy had told her he'd built it a couple of years ago. Now, their mother, Cynthia Murdock, lived there with her son.

"I guess Susan will be moving in soon," she said, very much aware of Dillon's obvious scorn for the elegant brick house with the lavish landscaping.

"I guess so," Dillon replied, his gaze reflecting the timid moonlight covering them like a fine mist. "Hope she can stand the squeaky clean linoleum and all the gadgets and gizmos my brother had installed."

"It's probably more convenient for your mother, at least," Isabel said, trying to be tactful.

Dillon scoffed again. "Yeah, well, Eli always did have Mother's best interest at heart."

He turned then, his eyes moving over the old plantation house. He stood stoic and still, then said in a voice soft with regret, "I miss this house. I wanted to come home to *this* house."

Isabel's heart went out to him. Dillon, always the wild child, always the scrapper, getting into trouble, getting into jams that his father and older brother had had to pull him out of. Dillon, the son who'd left in a huff, mad at the world in general, and hadn't looked back. Now, he was home, for whatever reason.

Isabel could feel sympathy for whatever Dillon Murdock was experiencing. He'd had it all handed to him. His life had been so easy, so perfect. And what had he done? Thrown it all back in his parents' faces. What she would have given to have been able to live with that kind of security, with that kind of protection. But instead, she'd had to live in a house so full of holes, the winter wind had chilled her to the bone each night as she'd lain underneath piles of home-made quilts. She'd had to live in a house with run-down plumbing and a leaky roof, simply because the Murdocks didn't deem her family good enough for repairs. They lived in the house for free; what more did they want anyway? That had been the consensus, as far as the Murdocks were concerned. No, she couldn't feel sorry for Dillon Murdock. Yet she did, somehow. And that made her put up her guard.

"I always loved this house," she said now as she strolled over to the raised porch of the mansion. Swinging her slight frame up onto the splintered planks, she sat staring out into the night, into Dillon Murdock's eyes. "It's a shame it has to stand empty. Some people don't realize what they have, obviously."

She hadn't meant the statement to sound so bitter, but she could see Dillon hadn't missed the edge in her words. He came to stand in front of her, his eyes lifting to meet hers. "You're right there. It took me a long time to learn that lesson."

Isabel studied him, searching for clues of the life he must have led. But Dillon's face was as hard as granite, blank and unflinching, unreadable. Until she looked into his eyes. There, she saw his soul, raw and battered, his eyes as aged and gray as the wood underneath the peeling paint of this old house.

"So, you've come home," she said, accepting that

he didn't owe her any explanations. Accepting that she didn't need, or want, to get involved with the Murdocks' personal differences.

Dillon stepped so close, she could see the glint of danger in his eyes, could feel the warmth of his breath fanning her hair away from her face. His nearness caused a fine row of goose bumps to go racing down her bare arms, in spite of the warm spring night. Yet, she didn't dare move. She just sat there, holding her breath, hoping he'd back away. But he didn't.

"We've both come home, Isabel," he observed as he leaned against the aging porch. "But the question is, what have we come home to?"

With that, he turned and stalked away into the night, leaving her to wonder if she'd made the right decision after all. Taking a deep breath, she pushed her hair away from her face and wondered if maybe she should have stayed away from Wildwood a little longer. Well, she was here now. But while she was here, she'd be sure to stay clear of Dillon Murdock.

She didn't like feeling sorry for him. She didn't like feeling anything for him.

Yet, she did. Even after all these years, she still did.

Chapter Two

The smell of homemade cinnamon rolls greeted Isabel as she entered the screened back door of the old farmhouse. Grammy had already set the table, complete with fresh flowers from her garden. Touching her hand to a bright orange Gerber daisy, Isabel closed her eyes for just a minute. It was good to be home, in spite of her feelings regarding Wildwood. The meeting with Dillon had left her shaken and unsure, but being here with Grammy gave her strength and security. Grammy always made things seem better.

"There you are," an aged voice called from the arched doorway leading to the long narrow kitchen off to the right. "I was getting worried."

Isabel set her camera down on a nearby rickety side table, then stepped forward to take the two glasses of iced tea from her grandmother's plump, veined hands. "Sorry, Grammy. I got carried away taking pictures of the wildflowers."

She didn't mention that she'd also gotten carried away with seeing Dillon Murdock again. She wasn't ready to discuss him with her grandmother.

"You and that picture taking," Martha said, waving a hand, her smile gentle and indulging. "The flowers are sure pretty right now, though." Settling down onto the puffy cushion of her cane-backed chair, she added, "Miss Cynthia always did love her wildflowers. I remember one time a few years back, that Eli got it in his head to mow them down. Said they were an eyesore, what with the old house closed up and everything."

"He didn't do it, did he?" Isabel asked, her eyes going wide. "That would have ruined them."

Martha chuckled as she automatically reached for Isabel's hand, prepared to say grace. "Oh, no. He tried, though. Had one of the hired hands out on a mower early one morning. Miss Cynthia heard the tractor and went tramping through the flowers, all dressed in a pink suit and cream pumps, her big white hat flapping in the wind. She told that tractor driver to get his hide out of her flowers. She watched until that poor kid drove that mower clear back to the equipment barn. Then she headed off, prim as ever, to her Saturday morning brunch at the country club."

Isabel shook her head, sat silently as Grammy said grace, then took a long swallow of the heavily sweetened tea. "I was right. Some things never change."

Martha passed her the boiled new potatoes and fresh string beans. "Do you regret taking the Murdocks up on their offer?"

Isabel bit into a mouthful of the fresh vegetables,

then swallowed hastily. "You mean being the official photographer for Eli's extravagant wedding?"

"I wouldn't use the same wording, exactly," Martha said, a wry smile curving her wrinkled lips, "but I reckon that's what I was asking."

Smiling, herself, at her grandmother's roundabout way of getting to the heart of any matter, Isabel stabbed her knife into her chicken-fried steak, taking out her frustrations on the tender meat. "Well, I'm having second thoughts, yes," she admitted, her mind on Dillon. "But I couldn't very well turn them down. They're paying me a bundle and I can always use the cash. But, I mainly did it because you asked me to, Grammy."

"Don't let me talk you into anything," Martha said, her blue eyes twinkling.

"As if you've ever had to talk anyone into anything," Isabel responded, laughing at last. "You could sweet-talk a mule into tap dancing."

"Humph , never tried that one." Her grandmother grinned impishly. "But I did bake your favorite cinnamon rolls, just in case—Miss Mule."

"For dessert?" Isabel asked, sniffing the air, the favorite nickname her grandmother always used to imply that she was stubborn slipping over her head. "Or do I have to hold out till breakfast?"

Martha reached across the lacy white tablecloth to pat her granddaughter's hand. "Not a soul here, but you and me. Guess we can eat 'em any time we get hungry for 'em."

"Dessert, then, definitely," Isabel affirmed, munching down on her steak. "Ah, Grammy, you are the best cook in the world."

"Well, you could have my cooking a lot more if you came to visit more often."

Isabel set her fork down, her gaze centered on her sweet grandmother. She loved her Grammy; loved her plump, sweet-scented welcoming arms, loved her smiling, jovial face, loved her gray tightly curled hair. Yet, she couldn't bring herself to move back here permanently, a subject they'd tossed back and forth over the years.

Her tone gentle, she said, "Grammy, don't start with that. You know I have to travel a lot in my line of work and I don't always have an opportunity to come home."

Martha snorted. "Well, you told me yourself you didn't have any assignments lined up over the next few weeks, so you can stay here and have a nice vacation. Living in a suitcase—that is no kind of life for a young lady."

"I have an apartment in Savannah."

"That you let other people live in—what kind of privacy does that give you?"

"Very little, when I manage to get back there," Isabel had to admit. "Subletting is the only way to hold on to it, though."

"And you always going on and on when you were little about having a home of your own."

Her appetite suddenly gone, Isabel stared down at the pink-and-blue-flowered pattern on her grandmother's aged china. "Yeah, I did do that. But I never got that home. And I've learned to be content with what I do have." Only lately, she had to admit, her nomadic life was starting to wear a little thin.

Wanting to lighten the tone of the conversation, she

jumped up to hug her grandmother. "And I have everything I need—like home-baked cinnamon rolls and a grandmother who doesn't nag too much."

Martha sighed and patted Isabel's back, returning the hug generously. "Okay, Miss Mule, I can take a hint. I won't badger you anymore—tonight at least."

"Thank you," Isabel said, settling back down in her own chair. "Now, how 'bout one of those rolls you promised me?"

"Glad to be home?" Martha challenged, her brows lifting, a teasing glow on her pink-cheeked face.

"Oh, all right, yes," Isabel admitted, taking the small defeat as part of the fun of having a remarkable woman for a grandmother. "I'm glad to be home."

"That's good, dear."

Isabel smiled as Martha headed into the kitchen to retrieve two fat, piping hot cinnamon rolls. Martha Landry was a pillar of the church, a Sunday school teacher who prided herself on teaching the ways of Jesus Christ as an example of character and high moral standing, but with a love and practicality that reached the children much more effectively than preaching down to them ever could.

Isabel knew her grandmother wouldn't preach to her, either; not in the way her own parents always had. It was a special part of her relationship with her grandmother that had grown over the years since her parents' deaths. She could talk to Grammy about anything and know that Martha Landry wouldn't sit in judgment. One of Grammy's favorite Bible quotes was from First Corinthians: "For if we would judge ourselves, we should not be judged."

Isabel knew her grandmother believed in accepting

people as humans, complete with flaws. And that included their mighty neighbors. Yet Isabel couldn't
help but judge the Murdocks, since they'd passed
judgment on her a long time ago.

"I saw Dillon tonight," she said now, her gaze
locking with her grandmother's, begging for understanding. "He's home for the wedding."

Isabel watched for her grandmother's reaction, and
seeing no condemnation, waited for Martha to speak.

"Well, well," the older woman said at last, her
carefully blank gaze searching Isabel's face. "And
how was Mr. Dillon Murdock?"

"Confused, I believe," Isabel replied. "He seemed
so sad, Grammy. So very sad."

"That man's had a rough reckoning over the past
few years. From what I've heard, he hasn't had it so
easy since he left Wildwood."

Hating herself for being curious, Isabel asked,
"And just what did you hear?"

Grammy feigned surprise. "Child, you want me to
pass on gossip?"

Isabel grinned. "Of course not. I just want you to
share what you know."

Martha licked sweet, white icing off her fingers.
"Yep, you want me to spill the beans on Dillon Murdock. Do you still have a crush on him, after all these
years?"

Isabel cringed at her grandmother's sharp memory,
then sat back to try to answer that question truthfully.
"You know, Grammy, I had a crush on him, true.
But that was long ago, and even though I saw Dillon
each and every day, I never really knew him. And I

don't know him now. It was a dream, and not a very realistic one.''

"Amen to that. And now?''

Isabel couldn't hide the truth from her grand-mother. "And now, I'm curious about the man he's become. Seeing him again tonight, well, it really threw me. He seemed the same, but he also seemed different. I'm hoping he's changed some.''

Martha gave her a long, scrutinizing stare. "That's all well and good, honey. But remember, the boy you knew had problems, lots of problems. And as far as we know, the man might still be carrying those same problems. I'd hate to see you open yourself up to a world of hurt.''

Isabel got up to clear away their dishes, her eyes downcast. "Oh, you don't have to worry on that account, Grammy. When I left Wildwood, I promised myself I'd never be hurt by the Murdocks again.''

"Including Dillon?''

"Especially Dillon,'' Isabel readily retorted. Then she turned at the kitchen door. "Although Dillon never really did anything that terrible to me.''

"Oh, really?''

"Really. Oh, he teased me a lot, but mostly his only fault was that he was a Murdock. Eli, on the other hand, made no bones about my being the poor hired help. I just can't tolerate their superior attitudes and snobbery. Not now. I did when I was living here, but not now. Not anymore.''

Martha followed Isabel into the kitchen. "And did Mr. Dillon Murdock act superior tonight, when you talked to him?''

Isabel surprised herself by defending him. "No, he didn't. Not at all. In fact, he was…almost humble."

"I just hope that boy's learned from his mistakes."

"Me, too," Isabel said. "Me, too."

Dillon's soul-weary eyes came back to her mind, so brilliantly clear, she had to shake her head to rid herself of the image. "You don't have to worry about me and Dillon Murdock, Grammy. I don't plan on falling for any of his sob stories."

"Should be an interesting wedding," Martha commented, her hands busy washing out plates.

Isabel didn't miss the implications of that statement. She never could fool her grandmother.

Dillon stood at the back door of his brother's house, every fiber of his being telling him not to enter the modern, gleaming kitchen. But his mother was standing at the sink, dressed in white linen slacks and a blue silk blouse, her curled hair turned now from blond to silver-white, her small frame more frail-looking than Dillon remembered. He smiled as he heard her loudly giving orders to the maid who'd been with their family for years.

"Now, Gladys, we want everything to be just right, remember? So finish up there, dear, then you can go on back to tidying the guest room for Dillon. He'll be here any minute."

Cynthia had written to him, begging him to come home for his brother's wedding.

And so here he stood.

The minute he opened the glass door to the room, he was assaulted with the scent of dinner rolls baking, along with the scent of fragrant potpourri and a trace of his mother's overly sweet perfume. At least some parts of Eli's new home were familiar.

"Hello, Mama," he said from his spot by the door.

Cynthia whirled from directing the maid to see who'd just entered her kitchen, her gray eyes wide, her mouth opening as she recognized her younger son. "Oh, my...Dillon. You came home."

Dillon took his tiny mother into his arms, his hands splaying across her back in a tight hug, his eyes closing as memories warmed his heart even while it broke all over again. Then he set his mother away, so he could look down into her face. "This isn't my home, Mother. Not this house. It belongs to Eli."

"Well, you're welcome here. You should know that," Cynthia insisted as she reached up to push a stubborn spike of hair away from his forehead. "You look tired, baby."

He was tired. Tired of worrying, wondering, hoping, wishing. He didn't want to be here, but he wanted to be with his mother. She was getting older. They'd kept in touch, but he should have come home long ago. "I could use a glass of tea," he said by way of hiding what he really needed. "Where's Eli?"

"Right here," his brother said from a doorway leading into the airy, spacious den. "Just got in from the cotton patch." Stomping into the kitchen, his work boots making a distinctive clicking sound, Eli Murdock looked his brother over with disdain and contempt. "Of course, you wouldn't know a thing about growing cotton, now would you, little brother?"

"Not much," Dillon admitted, a steely determination making him bring his guard up.

His brother had aged visibly in the years that Dillon had been away. Eli's hair was still thick and black, but tinges of gray now peppered his temples. He was still tall and commanding, but his belly had a definite paunch. He looked worn-out, dusty, his brown eyes shot with red.

"So, it's cotton now?" Dillon asked by way of conversation. "When did we switch cash crops? I thought corn and peanuts were our mainstay."

"*We* didn't do anything," Eli said as he poured himself a tall glass of water then pointed at his own chest. "I, little brother, I did all the work on this farm, while you were gallivanting around Atlanta, living off Daddy's money. Why'd you come back, anyway—to beg Mama for your inheritance?"

"Eli!" Cynthia moved between her sons with practiced efficiency. "I invited Dillon home, for your wedding. And I want you to try to be civil to each other while he's here. Do you both understand?"

Dillon looked at his mother's hopeful, firm expression, then glanced at the brooding hostility on his brother's ruddy face. "Why don't you ask the groom, Mother?"

"I'm asking both of you," Cynthia said, her eyes moving from one son to the other. "For my sake, and for Susan's sake."

Eli hung his head, then lifted his gaze to Dillon. "As long as he stays out of my way. I won't have him ruining Susan's big day."

"Thoughtful of you," Dillon countered. "But, hey, I won't if you won't, brother."

"I'll be too preoccupied with my bride to pay you

any attention," Eli retorted, a distinct smugness in his words.

Wanting to counter his lack of tact, Dillon said, "Well, it certainly took you long enough to find a woman willing to put up with you."

That hit home. Eli set his glass down, then placed both hands on his hips. "I don't see you bringing any young ladies home to meet Mama."

Cynthia clapped her hands for quiet. "Enough of this. Can we please sit down to have a pleasant dinner together? Gladys and I made baked catfish and squash casserole."

"Why did you have to invite him back here?" Eli asked. "And for my wedding, of all things?"

"I wanted your brother here," Cynthia said, tears glistening her eyes. "I wanted my sons to make peace with each other."

Eli stomped to the sink to wash his hands and face. Then turning to dry himself with a dish towel, he said, "I don't have to make peace with Dillon, Mama. He's the one who should be doing the apologizing. He ran off."

"No, you drove me off," Dillon said, then he turned to his mother. "I'm sorry, I can't stay in this house. I'll be at the wedding, Mama, and I'll show up at all the required functions, but if you need me, I'll be at Wildwood."

"You can't stay in that run-down house," Cynthia said, grabbing his arm as he headed for the door.

"I'll be fine."

"Let him go," Eli called. "Let him try to survive in this heat, with no water or electricity. He'll be back across the road soon enough."

Dillon gently extracted himself from his mother's fierce grip. "I'll see you later, Mama."

"That's just like you," Eli said. "Turn and run again. You never could stick around long enough to do any good around here."

"Eli, hush," Cynthia said. Then she called to Dillon, "I'll bring you a warm plate over later."

Dillon just kept walking, and he didn't stop until he reached the wildflower field. Then he fell down on his knees and stared up into the starry sky. He wanted to get on his motorcycle and ride away. But, this time, something held him back. This time, Isabel's green eyes and sweet-smelling hair haunted him and held him while her words came back to taunt him.

What are you doing back here?

Maybe it was time he found the answer to that question.

Maybe this time, he *would* stay and fight.

The next morning, Isabel remembered just how interesting things could become in a small town. The wedding of one of the most eligible, elusive bachelors in the county was the talk of the small hamlet, so everyone who was anyone would be invited to the event. And those who weren't invited would bust a gut trying to hear the details.

Isabel was scheduled to meet Susan Webster at the bridal shop on Front Street at ten o'clock. Susan's mother wanted Isabel to see Susan in the dress, then they'd decide where to start taking the preliminary pictures of the bride in all her splendor.

Pulling her rented Jeep up to the curve of the Brides and Beaus formal wear shop, Isabel got the strange sense that the curious townspeople were watching *her* return closely, too.

"Guess I'm a strange creature," she told Susan after hugging the other woman. "The radical free spirit comes home to Wildwood."

"We gave that particular honor to Dillon," Susan said, her bright blue eyes lighting up in spite of the wisecrack. "Did you know he's moved back in the old house? Opened up a couple of rooms. He refuses to stay in Eli's house."

Hoping she didn't sound too interested, Isabel tossed her long braid aside and shrugged. "Dillon always was a loner."

"Understatement," Susan replied, dragging Isabel into the back of the long, cluttered shop. Past the pastel formals and tuxedos that went flying off the racks at prom time, they entered the bride room where Susan's plump mother, Beatrice, sat going over the final details of the bridesmaid dresses with a clerk.

"Hello, Isabel," Beatrice said, smiling up at her. "Isn't this exciting? My baby's finally getting married, and to Eli Murdock. I'm so proud."

"It is exciting, Mrs. Webster," Isabel replied, bending down to hug the older woman. She'd have to be careful about keeping her real feelings regarding this match to herself. "And I'm touched that you both wanted me to be a part of it."

"Wait until you see the dress," Beatrice enthused, her attention already back on her job as mother of the bride.

"Wow, look at all this lace and satin," Isabel quipped, holding a hand to her eyes as she looked around at all the dresses and veils hanging in the prim room. "So bright and so white."

"Still wedding shy, I see," Susan said, sweeping around with her arms wrapped to her chest. "Not me, Isabel. I'm very happy."

Isabel eyed her high school friend, wanting desperately to ask her how she'd fallen for a cold fish like Eli Murdock. But she wouldn't dream of saying anything to hurt kind, gentle Susan. "You look sickeningly happy," she told Susan, her smile genuine. "You were meant to be married."

"Took me long enough to notice Eli, though," Susan said as they settled down on a cushioned sofa. "Imagine, all those years in the same town, then one day we ran into each other at the Feed and Seed...."

"Very romantic," Isabel said, grinning. "Tell me, did it happen over the corn seeds or maybe the... er...manure pile."

"Oh, you!" Susan laughed, then patted Isabel's hand. "I'm so glad you'll be taking the pictures. I insisted, you know. I told them you were nationally famous and we might not be able to get you for such a frivolous assignment, so I convinced Eli to pay you big bucks."

Isabel didn't hide her surprise. "Well, that explains a few things. I couldn't understand why the Murdocks wanted me so badly."

"Oh, they do," Susan assured her, her face flushing. "I mean, Mrs. Murdock agreed wholeheartedly—"

Seeing the other woman's embarrassment, Isabel shrugged again. "I understand, Susan. Eli wasn't too keen on the idea of hiring me to take your wedding pictures, huh?''

"I can explain that," Susan began, clearly appalled that she'd let that little tidbit out.

"No need," Isabel replied. "Eli and I never did see eye to eye. But that's all in the past. And if the request came from you, then I accept completely, and...I don't mind taking some of Eli's money off his hands. Now, show me this dress everyone keeps raving about.''

Ever the excited bride, Susan hopped up. "It's so beautiful!" Then she turned to stare down at Isabel, a troubled look on her pretty features. "Eli's changed, Isabel. Really, he has.''

"I know you wouldn't marry him if you didn't believe that, Susan," Isabel replied softly. "And I do hope you'll always be as happy as you look right now.''

Just to prove her point, she snapped a picture of Susan. And captured the tad of sadness she saw flickering quickly through the girl's eyes. Had Eli already started causing worry to his young bride?

"Susan," she asked as she watched her friend chatting with one of the clerks, "you'd tell me if anything was wrong, right?''

Susan whirled around, her features puzzled. "Wrong? What could be wrong?" Then lowering her head, she sighed, "It's just...I'm so excited I haven't been able to eat or sleep. I'm so in love, Isabel." With that, Susan was off to the dressing room to put on her elaborate bride dress.

Not good at waiting, Isabel got up to saunter around the shop. She'd brought her own gown to wear to the wedding, but some of the dresses offered here were quite lovely. Remembering her first prom, she balked as a vision of a young Dillon in his prom tuxedo, with a popular cheerleader encased in satiny pink by his side, came to mind. Isabel's dress that night had been homemade, an inexpensive knockoff made from a pattern with some gaudy material her mother had found on sale.

It had been Dillon's senior year, but Isabel had still been a junior in high school. Dillon had teased Isabel about her date, a football player who had a reputation for taking advantage of young girls' hearts, then later that night Dillon had asked Isabel to dance with him. She'd promptly refused, too afraid of her own mixed feelings to get near him. And too obsessed with Dillon to let the football player make any moves on her.

"Get over it, Isabel," she told herself now as she watched a bright-eyed teenager drooling over the many formal dresses crushed together all around them like delicate flower buds. She refused to think about Dillon Murdock.

But when the front door of the shop opened and the man himself stepped into the room, she had no choice but to acknowledge him. His masculine presence filled the dainty store with a bold, daring danger. And his eyes on her only added to the rising temperature of the humid summer day.

"Dillon," she said, too breathlessly.

"Isabel." He strode toward her, his eyes twinkling with amusement. "I see they've put you straight to work."

"Yes. I'm here to get a few shots of Susan in her

dress and to set up a more formal location for her portrait shots."

He nodded, then ran his fingers through his hair. "Mama wanted me to get fitted for a tux. I tried to get out of it, but—" His shrug was indifferent.

The image of him in a tuxedo made Isabel want to drool just like a teenager. But she quickly reprimanded herself, and putting on a blank expression, said, "But your mother persuaded you to come in anyway."

He nodded, a wry grin slicing his angular face. "You know the woman well."

Isabel wanted to remind him that she knew all the Murdocks very well. Well enough to be wary of any association with them. Instead she asked, "How is your mother?"

Dillon hesitated, then decided to keep his family problems to himself, not that it mattered. The whole town would probably soon be talking about his renewed feud with his brother, and the fact that he'd moved into the run-down plantation house.

He shrugged. "You know Mama. She's tough. And she's okay, I reckon. Stressed about this wedding."

And probably about having him back home, no doubt, Isabel decided.

Just then a nervous female clerk came forward. "Mr. Murdock, I'm Stacey Whitfield. If you'll just follow me, we can have you fitted in no time."

"Thanks, Stacey," Dillon said with a winning smile. "Give me a minute, all right?"

The fascinated woman bobbed her head, then hurried to stand behind the counter, her eyes glued to Dillon and Isabel.

Dillon fingered a bit of lace on a nearby sleeve while the teenaged shopper Isabel had noticed earlier now had her wide eyes centered on *him* rather than a new frock. Isabel watched in detached amusement as the young girl's mother shooed her out the door, the woman's look of disapproval apparent for all to see.

"My reputation precedes me," Dillon observed on a flat note. "Mothers, lock up your daughters. He's back in town."

"Should they be worried?" Isabel asked, all amusement gone now.

· "No," he replied as he came closer, his hand moving from the trailing lace to a strand of curling hair at her temple. "But maybe *you* should be."

Her breath caught in her throat, but she stared him down anyway, challenging him with a lift of her chin. "Why me?"

He leaned closer. "Because if I chase after anybody while I'm here, it'll be you, Isabel. We've got a lot of catching up to do."

Snatching his hand away, Isabel busied herself with checking her camera. "I don't have time for catching up, Dillon. I'm only here as a favor to Susan and my grandmother."

"Right."

"I'm serious."

"So am I."

Angry at herself more than him, she snapped, "You can stop playing games with me, Dillon. I'm not the naive young girl I used to be. And I won't be taunted and teased by a Murdock, ever again."

Clearly shocked at the venom in her words, Dillon backed away. "I guess I didn't realize you could hold such a grudge. But you're right. And wise to stay away from the likes of me.'' Turning to stalk toward the door, he called to the confused clerk waiting to take his measurements, ''I'll be back later, Stacey. It's a little too confining in here right now.''

With that, he slammed the front door, leaving a stunned silence to follow him, and all eyes clearly on Isabel.

Chapter Three

She refused to feel guilty about what she'd said to Dillon. The man needed to know right off the bat that she wasn't interested.

But, she reluctantly told herself, Dillon had looked so dejected, so hurt when she'd accused him of taunting her. She'd seen it in his stormy eyes just before he'd shut down on her. Then, he'd warned her away, as surely as he'd tried to draw her near. Now the whole town would probably be talking about the little scene in the bridal shop.

When Isabel went into the back with Stacey to tell Susan that Dillon had left, the bride-to-be was clearly flustered.

"What do you mean, he left?" a frazzled Susan asked poor embarrassed Stacey. "We have to fit him for that tuxedo!"

Stacey shuffled her loafered feet and looked over to Isabel for support. "He...he was talking to Isabel and he—"

"Dillon couldn't wait," Isabel explained, shooing Stacey away with the wave of her hand. Turning Susan back around to view herself in the three-way mirror, she commented on the exquisite bridal dress. "This is incredible, Susi."

Looking over her silk-and-lace reflection, Susan soon forgot all about Dillon's leaving. "Do you like it?"

"I do," Isabel said, although she herself would have chosen a more understated wedding gown. All that pearl beading and lace seemed a bit overwhelming. But then, she reminded herself, she wasn't the one getting married. "I knew you'd make a lovely bride. Now, let me just get a few candid shots of you here, and then we can talk about the formal portrait for the newspaper. You know, I thought about the wildflowers. How would you feel about setting up a shoot there?"

Susan's excitement changed to worry in the blink of her blue eyes. Looking over at her mother for support, she said, "Oh, I don't know—Eli hates those flowers. He calls them weeds."

Mrs. Webster fussed with Susan's veil, then nodded. "It's true, Isabel. Eli doesn't like the wildflower patch. It's been a bone of contention between him and his mother for some time now."

Susan lowered her voice to a whisper. "Something about it being Dillon's favorite spot—"

"What?" Isabel raked a hand through her long hair to keep from saying something she'd regret.

"Couldn't we do it somewhere else?" Susan questioned, her blue eyes big and round. "How about in the garden behind Eli's house? He had it especially landscaped—that big nursery from Albany did it. They did such a good job, too.''

The image Isabel had of Susan in her wedding gown amid the wildflowers died on the vine. Eli certainly wouldn't want his bride centered in a field that only reminded him of his unwelcome brother. Remembering how lonely Dillon had looked the night before, she couldn't help the little tug of regret in her heart. Maybe she shouldn't have been so nasty to Dillon earlier.

Reminding herself she was being paid to please the bride *and* the groom, and that she had to stand firm regarding Dillon Murdock, she nodded. ''If that's what you want, of course, we can do the shoot there. But Eli can't see you in your dress, remember?''

''Oh, no.'' Susan's big eyes widened. ''That'd be bad luck and we don't need any more of that.''

Curious, Isabel asked, ''Have you had some problems?''

Beatrice Webster pursed her lips, then started to speak.

Susan hastily shook her head to stop her mother, then gazed at her reflection in the mirror, her eyes glistening. ''No, everything's fine. It's just that Eli has this cotton crop to worry about, and well, he works so hard. And now, Dillon's already started showing himself. I won't have him ruining my wedding, Isabel, I just won't. We only invited him back because his poor mama wanted him here for his brother's wedding, and he doesn't even have the common decency to try on his tuxedo.''

Isabel stopped snapping pictures to stare up at her friend. ''Susan, Dillon left the shop because of me.

We…we kind of got into a little argument and I'm afraid I was rude to him. I'll try to smooth things over with him, I promise."

Clearly relieved, Susan clapped her hands together, her number one concern right now her wedding. "Would you please try to get him back in here, tomorrow morning if possible? We've only got a few days left before the rehearsal supper, then the wedding."

"I promise," Isabel said, dreading the whole affair all over again. She must have been crazy to even accept this assignment.

An hour later, she found herself in the wildflower field, amid the honeybees and the butterflies, dreading having to see Dillon again. But she had to apologize and persuade him to do his duty. A promise was a promise, and she *had* caused him to leave the shop.

Only she didn't run into Dillon in the field. Instead, she saw his petite mother hurrying across the path, a huge plate covered with a white linen napkin balanced on her wrinkled hands.

"Miss Cynthia," Isabel called, rushing to help the woman with the heavily laden plate. "My goodness, you've got enough food here to feed an army!"

"Isabel! I heard you made it in. Susan's mother— that woman calls me at least three times a day." Cynthia stopped to take a long, much needed breath. "How are you, dear?"

Isabel dutifully leaned down to kiss the woman's rosy powdered cheek, noting that Miss Cynthia was dressed impeccably just to cross the road and tramp through a field. She wore a pink cotton shell, pearls, and dressy gray slacks with matching pumps.

"I'm all right, Miss Cynthia. Do you want me to carry that for you?"

Cynthia shifted the platter, then laughed nervously. "Heavens, no. I'm just in a hurry. Eli will be home soon, and I'll have to answer to him. He doesn't want me carting food over here to his brother."

Isabel hurried along with Miss Cynthia. "Just like you used to do—sneaking Dillon food after he got sent to bed with no supper."

"I'm just an old softy, aren't I?" Cynthia said, her sharp eyes moving over Isabel. "My, you've changed. You've turned out to be quite a lovely young lady, Isabel."

"Still a little tomboy left, though," Isabel said, remembering how Cynthia Murdock used to encourage her to wash her face and put on some makeup. Isabel had resented the woman's heavy-handed suggestions at the time, but now she only smiled. Apparently, Beatrice Webster hadn't wasted any time updating the whole town on Isabel's improved grooming habits. Straightening the flowing skirt of her soft linen dress, she told Miss Cynthia, "I did remember some of your fashion tips."

"I can tell," Cynthia agreed as they reached the back porch of the old mansion. "That red sundress is mighty fetching with your blond hair."

Fetching. Only Cynthia Murdock could use an old-fashioned word like that and make it sound classy and completely perfect. But the woman could also cut people into ribbons with a few well-chosen words, Isabel remembered.

"Let me get the door," Isabel said now without thinking.

The two women were busy laughing and talking as they entered the long central hallway of the cool, shuttered house. Which is why they didn't see the man standing at the end of the long kitchen, splashing water from an aluminum bucket sitting on the wash drain all over his face and bare chest, until it was too late to back out of the room.

Dillon heard the commotion, then looked up to find his mother and Isabel standing there in the doorway, looking at him as if he were doing something scandalous.

"I didn't hear a knock," he said, his lazy gaze moving from his shocked mother's face to the stunning woman standing beside her. "And I don't recall inviting two pretty ladies to dinner."

Cynthia quickly got over her shock and set the heavy platter on the cracked counter. "I found Isabel walking through the wildflowers. And…there's plenty enough here for two."

Dillon didn't bother to hide his bare chest, or the surprise his mother's bold suggestion brought to his face. "Mama, are you trying to fix me up with our Isabel?"

Cynthia snorted. "I was trying to cover up for your lack of manners, son. Where is your shirt, anyway?"

"Over there." He pointed to a suitcase tossed carelessly up on one of the many long counters. "Throw me one, will you, Isabel?"

Gritting her teeth, and pulling her eyes back inside her head, Isabel chose a plain white T-shirt to hurl at him, her small grunt of pleasure indicating that she wished it had been something that could do a little more damage.

Dillon caught the shirt, his eyes still on Isabel. With lazy disregard, he pulled it over his damp hair, then tucked it into the equally damp waistband of his jeans. "Sorry, Mama, but I didn't know I'd have an audience for my bath. Guess it's a good thing I kept my breeches on."

Cynthia threw up her hands. "He's still a charmer, isn't he, Isabel?"

"Oh, he is indeed." Isabel turned to leave. "And I really can't stay. I just wanted to say hello, Miss Cynthia."

Dillon leaned across the old, planked table standing in the middle of the kitchen. "What's your hurry?"

Isabel turned to see him reclining there, bathed in a golden shaft of afternoon sunlight, his gray eyes almost black with a teasing, challenging light.

She wanted to take his picture again. But she wouldn't, because she wasn't going to stay in this hot room any longer. She'd just have to figure out some other way of getting him to cooperate with Susan about that tuxedo. If she stayed here right now, she couldn't be sure she'd be in control of her wayward feelings.

Tossing back a long strand of hair, she said, "Actually, I was taking pictures and I ran into your mother. I didn't mean to disturb you."

Cynthia cleared her throat and shooed Isabel back into the room. "Stay and talk to my son, please. Maybe you can convince him to come over to Eli's house, where there's plenty of fresh water and air-conditioning."

Isabel hesitated, her gaze locking with Dillon's. "I

don't think it's my place to argue with your son, Miss Cynthia."

"And why?" Cynthia questioned with a diamond bejeweled hand on her hip. "You two used to argue all the time. That boy used to send you running, nearly in tears. But only after you'd given him a good piece of your mind."

Isabel lowered her head to stare at a crack in the pine flooring. "Well, that was then—"

"And this is now," Dillon finished. "Mama's right. I'm not minding my manners. Stay and talk to me a while, Isabel. I'll be on my best behavior, I promise."

"That's more like it," Miss Cynthia said, nodding her approval. "You two can keep each other company until we all get through this wedding."

Dillon lifted up off the table then to come around and kiss his mother. "Thanks, Mama. Now, you'd better get back. I suspect Eli doesn't know you've been feeding me."

"I'll take care of Eli, son."

"Yep, you always have, haven't you?"

Cynthia stopped at the wide doorway. "I'd be more than happy to take care of you, if you'd stay here long enough to let me."

Dillon's smile was bittersweet. "I'm fine, Mama. Really. Now, scoot."

Cynthia gave an eloquent shrug, then waved to Isabel. "Bye, now. Tell your grandmama hello for me, honey. Oh, and I might have some alterations to bring down to her next week. A couple of dresses that need taking in. I don't trust anybody else to do the job."

"I'll tell her," Isabel promised, thinking that as

always, Miss Cynthia had reminded her of her place. Her grandmother was still the hired help, no matter how fond Miss Cynthia was of Martha Landry. She waited until she heard the click of Miss Cynthia's heels on the back steps, then looked up at Dillon. "I'm not staying for supper, and I can see myself out."

He reached out a long tanned arm, catching her by the hand to hold her in her spot. "Was it something I said?"

She glanced back up to find his eyes centered on her with that questioning, brooding intensity. "No, Dillon. Actually, it was something *I* said. Susan is upset that you didn't get your fitting this morning. Will you just go back in tomorrow and get it over with?"

He dropped her arm to move to the red ice chest he had propped in one corner of the room. "Want a soda?"

"Okay," she said without giving it much thought. Just like she'd come bursting in here without much thought, to find him half-clothed. How she wished she'd knocked, but then, he probably would have come to the door bare-chested anyway. When he came back to hand her the icy cold can, she told herself she'd take a couple of sips then leave gracefully.

Then he pulled the white linen cover off the fried chicken. "Mmm, Mama does know how to fry up a chicken. Doesn't that smell so good?"

Her stomach growled like the traitor it was. Taking a bit of meat that Dillon tore from a crispy breast, she nibbled it, then tried to put the fat and calorie content out of her mind.

Unrolling the silverware his mother had thoughtfully provided, Dillon dipped a spoon into the white
mound beside the chicken, then held it out to Isabel.
"Want some mashed potatoes?"

"Stop it!" Isabel said, taking out her frustrations
on the pop top on her drink. The sound hissed and
sizzled almost as loudly as the tension between them.
"Just tell me you'll go back in and get your tux."

"I might," he said after shoveling the potatoes into
his own mouth. Then he picked up a drumstick and
bit into it. Chewing thoughtfully before he dropped it
back on the plate, his eyes on her, he said, "Then
again, I might just show up like this." He shrugged
and waved the white napkin over his jeans. "Or, I
might not show up at all."

That comment caused her to set her drink can down
with a thud. "Oh, that would be just perfect. Show
everyone around here that they're right about you after all. Make Susan feel even worse and cause your
mother even more heartache. Yeah, Dillon, I'd say
just blow the whole thing off. Why should you try to
do something for someone else, anyway?"

In a blur of motion, he dropped his napkin and
stood before her, one hand on her shoulder and one
braced on the panelled wall behind her. "Don't, Isabel. Don't make me feel any worse than I already
do."

She took a shuddering breath, her face inches from
his. "Why do you fight so hard against everything?"

His gaze traveled over her face, then back to her
eyes. "Why are you standing in my kitchen telling
me what I should or shouldn't be doing?"

She stared him down, though she knew she'd be a

nervous wreck later because of it. "Good question. So, let me go."

"No."

Glaring up at him, she said on a breath hot with rage, "You haven't changed a bit. Still the macho tough guy, still trying to make me feel small and insignificant."

He moved an inch closer. "Is that what I'm doing? Is that how you feel right now?"

She backed farther into the wall. "Yes, to both questions. I'm right up there on your list along with Eli and all the other people in this town you're still holding a grudge against, aren't I?"

"I thought you were the one with the grudge," he said, his hand lifting off her shoulder to come up and cup her chin. "You told me I'd never get to you again. Did I get to you before?"

"No," she said, hoping she'd be forgiven for lying. "No."

"Yes," he said. "Yes."

Then he lowered his mouth to hers and kissed her with a tenderness that contradicted everything she believed about him. No man this tough could kiss with such a whispered gentleness that it left a woman's soul dancing.

No man except Dillon, of course.

When he lifted his head, the kitchen was still and warm, the house silent and waiting. And his eyes were alive with a fire of surprise, of awe, of longing. "I wasn't teasing just now, Isabel."

Isabel swallowed hard, then tried to find what little sense of reason she had left. She shouldn't be here with him. She should run away as fast as she could.

Instead, she reached up a hand to stroke away that irresistible spike of hair centered on his forehead. "Are you sure, Dillon? Are you sure that kiss wasn't just a way to inflict pain on me?"

He ran a hand down the length of her hair, then gave her a wry smile. "Right now, darling, I'm not sure about anything, except that maybe I have a champion in you."

Surprised, she asked, "Why do you think that?"

He backed away then, letting her hair trail through his fingers to fall in cascading waves back around her shoulders. "Because, you *didn't* run away. You came here to fight me, and maybe, to fight for me. And you stayed even after I insulted you." Tipping his head to one side, his hands on his hips, he added, "And you stayed even after I kissed you."

Isabel moved away from the wall, and on shaking knees, tried to walk to the counter where she'd put her drink. Taking a long, cool swallow of the amber liquid, she turned to face him again. "I didn't have much choice. You had me against the wall."

A smug indifference replaced the gentleness she'd seen in his face. "That's how I court all of my women."

Tired and frightened of her own soaring feelings, she snapped at him. "We're not courting each other."

He came back strong. "Then what are we doing?"

Sighing, she threw her wavy hair back off her face, holding it tightly against her head with her hand. "I came here to ask you to behave, to show Susan some respect. But since it was my fault you left the shop this morning, I just wanted to make amends."

"Well, you did," he said, his voice going soft again. "You did that and a whole lot more."

Isabel dropped her hair over her shoulder, then crossed her arms over her chest in a defensive manner, still holding her soda with a loose hand. "Will you go back and get yourself a tux for the wedding?"

"Will you sit by me during the ceremony and dance with me at the reception?"

"I asked first."

"I'm asking now."

She smiled, then set her nearly empty can down. "You haven't changed a bit, Dillon."

He tipped a hand to his head in an acknowledging salute, then leaned back against the creaky table. "Ah, but you have. And for that, dear Isabel, I might be willing to behave—for my brother's wedding, that is."

"And wear the tux?" she said, tossing him the challenge.

"And wear the infernal tux," he added. Then he grabbed her to pull her back into his arms. "Just remember, save the last dance for me, okay?"

"Okay," she said as she allowed him to hold her close. Battling with Dillon Murdock had always left her drained.

Dillon didn't try to kiss her again. Instead, he just closed his eyes and held her. Isabel couldn't help feeling as if she'd come home. But she knew in her heart, that Dillon couldn't give her a home. Neither of them would linger here at Wildwood for very long. They were both still searching for something, some elusive something to ease the ache in their souls.

And all around them, the waning sun cascaded

through the tall kitchen windows in rays of gold, white and muted yellow, revealing dancing fragments of dust that had long lain as dormant and still as the pain buried deep in both their hearts.

Chapter Four

"**D**on't open the door!"

Isabel stood in the dark bathroom at the back of the house, watching through the red glow of the safe-light as the picture she'd taken of Dillon developed in a chemical bath. If her grandmother opened the door now, the picture would be ruined. "I'll be out in a minute, Grammy."

"It's not your grandma," a deep masculine voice said through the closed door.

Dillon.

Isabel almost knocked over her whole tray of developer. "Just a minute!" Taking a deep breath, she checked the timer, then stood back to see the emerging picture of the man who'd kissed her not two days ago, and who'd kept her awake thinking about him since then. With quick efficiency in spite of the flutter in her heart, she lifted the picture out of the developer, then dropped it in the stop bath for thirty seconds.

Another minute in the fixer, then a good wash for a couple of minutes, and the picture was done.

But the knocking at the door wasn't.

"Hey, you getting all dolled up or something?"

"Or something," Isabel retorted as she clipped the finished picture up on the clothesline she had extended across the cracked tub. "I'm working."

"Sorry, but that excuse won't wash. It's a pretty summer day and I have a hankering to take a walk down to the branch—with a pretty woman by my side."

Isabel stared at the picture of Dillon, her smile bittersweet. She'd captured his spirit as he stood there looking up at Wildwood. And somehow, since then, he was coming very close to capturing her heart. She'd have to be very careful about that. She wasn't ready to admit that Dillon had always held her heart.

Blinking, she called out, "Couldn't talk anyone else into it, huh?"

"Right. You seem to be the only woman around these parts willing to put up with me."

Opening the door just a fraction—she surely didn't want him to see that picture of himself—Isabel pasted an indulgent smile on her face. "You have such a unique way of asking a woman for a date, Dillon."

Dillon stood back in the small hallway, his eyes sweeping over her face, his half grin teasing and tempting. "And you, dear Isabel, sure have a way of looking as refreshing as a tall glass of lemonade. How do you do that?"

Ruffled, she lowered her head and crossed her arms around her chest, sure that she looked raggedy and drained from working in her makeshift darkroom all afternoon. Conscious of her faded cotton T-shirt and old shorts, she asked, "Do what?"

"You look different now, you know," he said instead of explaining himself. "I think it's the hair. You never wore it long before."

She left the bathroom and moved up the hall to the front of the rickety old house, running her hands through the swirls of loose curls falling away from her haphazard ponytail. "No, I didn't. Mama made me keep it cut. Said it was too much of a handful, what with all these waves and curls. I hated wearing it short."

He caught up with her in the kitchen. "So you let it grow."

"And grow," she said as she turned to hand him a glass of iced tea. "I guess it's silly, wearing it so long—"

"No, it suits you."

"Thank you," she said, acutely aware of his eyes on her. "I think it's probably more of a personal statement than a fashion decision."

"The rebellious daughter doing what her parents didn't approve of?"

She nodded, then lifted a brow. "Takes one to know one, I guess."

"I am one," he agreed. He set his now empty glass in the wide single sink and held out his hand. "C'mon, Issy, let's go for a long walk."

Stopping, Isabel stared across at him. "You called me Issy."

"Yeah, well, don't tell me you don't allow people to do that anymore."

"No, it's just that...no one besides you and my

immediate family even knows about that horrid nickname.''

"Issy, Issy, Issy," he teased, his grin widening.

Isabel's breath lifted right out of her body. She had forgotten what a lethal smile Dillon had. Maybe because she remembered his smiles being so rare. Coming up for air, she said, "Dilly, Dilly, Dilly," as a retort.

"Oh, boy. I should have never reminded you."

She took his hand in spite of all the name calling, very conscious of the rough calluses on his fingers. "I really need to finish developing that roll of film."

He gripped her fingers against his. "It'll keep."

He led her out the back door. The late afternoon air was ripe with the scents of early summer. Peaches growing fat on nearby trees, lilies blooming in her grandmother's carefully tended flower beds, roses drifting like rich cotton candy in the warm summer breeze. How could a woman resist such a day? Isabel believed God saved such days for special times, when people needed them the most.

She sure needed one. But with Dillon? How was she supposed to resist him and the sweet summer air, too?

"Who let you in, anyway?" she asked, looking around the yard for her grandmother.

He let go of her hand to turn and walk backward in front of her, much in the same way he used to do when they'd walk home after getting off the school bus. "I saw Martha on the road. She was headed to the Wedding War Room to help Mama with her dress. Told me to come and keep you company."

"How very thoughtful of my dear old grand-mother."

He gave her a sideways glance. "I thought so. Took her right up on her suggestion."

"Don't you have anything better to do?"

"I've made a few calls, done my work for the day."

Catching up to him, she asked, "And just what is your line of work these days?"

He turned serious then. "I run my own company, so I can set my own hours."

"Really?" Surprised at this revelation, she asked, "What sort of company?"

As smooth as the flattened red clay underneath their feet, he changed the subject. "I don't want to talk about work. I want to enjoy what's left of the day."

Isabel sensed his withdrawal, remembered it all too well from their years of growing up together. "Okay. You want to be irresponsible and play, right?"

He gave her that classic Dillon salute. "Right. It's what I do best, or so they tell me."

She didn't miss the sarcasm or the tinge of pain in his words. But she wouldn't press him to talk. That had been one of the things between them way back when, that is, when he hadn't been ribbing her or pestering her. Sometimes, they'd just sit quietly, staring off into nowhere together.

"Race you to the branch," she said, her long legs already taking off, her baggy walking shorts flying out around her knees.

Dillon was right on her heels. Just like always.

The branch was a shallow stream of clear, cool water that ran through a pine-shaded forest toward the back of the estate. The path to get there took them through the rows and rows of cotton just beginning to bud white on ruffly green vines.

"Eli and his cotton," Dillon said, the note of resentment in his voice echoing through the trees. "Our ancestors raised cotton on this land, but we quit growing it years ago. They say cotton's making a comeback, though. A good moneymaker, I reckon. And Eli sure likes his money."

"Is that so wrong?" Isabel questioned as she settled down on the same moss-covered bank she'd sat on as a child. "I mean, do you resent your family's wealth?"

Dillon snorted, then picked up a rock. With a gentle thud, he skipped it across the water, then plopped down beside her. "No, I don't resent my family's wealth. Thanks to my mother, I certainly spent my share of it before I settled down. It's just that Eli puts money and prominence before anything else."

"And you don't?"

"Not anymore."

Isabel glanced down at him, her heart skipping like the rock he'd thrown earlier. He looked so at home, lying there on a soft bed of pine straw in his faded jeans and Atlanta Braves T-shirt. She hadn't realized until this very moment how much she'd missed Dillon.

And he chose that very moment to look over at her, his eyes meeting hers in a knowing gaze that only reminded her of his kiss, his touch, his gentleness.

"You're pretty, Issy," he said, his voice as low and gravelly as the streambed.

To hide her discomfort, she said, "Don't sound so surprised."

"I am surprised," he admitted, his gaze moving over her face. "I don't remember you being so attractive."

No, he didn't remember much about her, Isabel thought. Even though he'd seen her every day of their growing up years, Dillon had taken her existence for granted. To him, she'd always be the poor kid next door. A fixture in his mind, just like his precious wildflower patch. Well, the wildflowers were the same. But she wasn't.

She looked away, out over the flowing water. "I don't remember me being so attractive, either. I was all legs and teeth."

"Not anymore," he said as he lifted up on his elbows. "I mean, you've still got legs, that's for sure, and when you smile—well, you have a pretty smile."

"Thank you, I think," she replied, her words lifting out over the breeze. "I guess the braces paid off after all." She took a long breath to retain some of her dignity. If she looked at him again—

"I like your lips, too."

That did it. "Dillon," she said, jumping up to move away, "are you deliberately flirting with me?"

He rolled over on his stomach, a lazy grin stretching across his swarthy face. "Well, of course. And if you come back over here, I intend to kiss you again."

She moved farther away. "No. We can't do this, Dillon."

"Why not?"

"You know why not."

He sat up then, brushing his hands together to scatter the pine needles he'd collected. "No, I honestly don't know why not. We're adults now, Issy. And no one can tell us what we can and can't do."

Isabel walked to the water's edge, then looked down at the sparkling stream where a school of tiny minnows danced in perfect symmetry. "But…we're still us, Dillon. I'm still the poor farm girl, and you're still the rich second son."

He came up in one fluid movement, then pulled her around to face him. "That's ridiculous. You can't still feel that way."

She looked up at him, wanting to touch him. But she didn't. "I do. Because it will never change. I wasn't ever good enough for you. And I never will be good enough for you."

Dillon's expression changed from perplexed to resolved. "I'm sorry, Issy. I never realized you wanted to be good enough for me. You see, I always thought it was the other way around."

"What do you mean?"

He came closer then, his eyes boring into her. "I always figured you didn't think I was worth your trouble. I never thought I was worthy of anybody's consideration around here."

Touched by his admission, Isabel reached a hand up to his face. "You never bothered to find out about me, Dillon. You never took the time to consider *me*."

Dillon stared down at her, seeing the hurt mixed with pride in her misty green eyes. If she only knew….

He placed his hand over hers, then brought their joined hands down between them. "Is that why you're fighting me now? You think I'm just playing with you, the same way I played with you when we were kids?''

"Well, aren't you?"

Dillon dropped her hand, then turned to stalk a few feet away, the honesty of touching her too much to bear just yet. Playing it cool, he chuckled. "Yeah, maybe I am, at that. Maybe I'm just bored and restless and, maybe I don't really want to be here." Shrugging, he said over his shoulder, "Yep, you sure got me all figured out."

Hearing the resentment, the anger, in his words only made her more determined to keep things clear between them. "I'm just being honest, Dillon. I didn't want to come back here, either. But I promised Grammy and Susan."

"That was noble of you."

Stomping over to him, her hands jammed into the deep pockets of her shorts, she said, "Look, I'm here for the same reasons you are. We're both here out of a sense of duty and obligation."

"Speak for yourself. As for me, I just wanted to come home—just for a little while."

Something, maybe that slight inflection in his voice that made him seem so vulnerable and lonely, brought her head up and made her want to understand him. "Because your mother asked you to, right?"

"Right. But, hey, everybody knows Dillon Murdock doesn't have a sense of obligation or honor. And I certainly don't know what duty means, now do I? I'm just bad ol' Dillon, enticing a pretty girl to the woods like the big bad wolf."

She'd wounded him. Somehow, she'd cracked that uncaring, cynical veneer. And what she saw there in the shimmering depths of his eyes tore her heart apart. "Dillon?"

He looked up just in time to see the sorrow in her eyes. "Don't, Isabel. Don't feel sorry for me. I don't want your pity."

"Dillon."

He lifted a hand to stop her from coming to him. "No, you're right, Isabel. This is a bad idea—you and me. You're right to have doubts about me." With that, he shrugged again, then gave her a bitter smile. "I guess I was just lonesome. I guess I just thought we could talk."

Completely confused, she said, "Then why did you tell me you wanted to kiss me again?"

"Just flirting," he said, his face blank, his tone indifferent. "Won't happen again."

"Okay," she said as she hurried to catch up with him. Behind them, the sun was snuggling up against the tree line. Another beautiful summer sunset. Isabel wished she had her camera. She also wished Dillon didn't walk so fast. "Listen, if you want to talk, that's fine—"

"I'm over it now," he said, his words curt and clipped. "I'll go on home and talk to myself."

Feeling smaller by the minute, she grabbed his arm. "Dillon, I mean it. I don't mind talking. And I'm a good listener."

He gave her a harsh laugh. "I've heard that line before, sweetheart."

"It's not a line. I...oh, I don't know what kind of games you're playing."

They were in the cotton patch now, moving down the dirt lane toward the main road. Off in the distance, the putter of a tractor's grinding motor vibrated through the field. But Dillon kept on walking.

Finally running to match his stride, Isabel yanked him by the arm. "Slow down, for goodness' sake."

He turned then to stumble into her arms, his eyes raking her face with longing and regret, while his hands gripped her elbows. "I gotta keep moving, Issy."

"Why?"

He lowered his head to hers. "Because if I stop, if I keep standing here with you in my arms, I'm gonna do something we'll both regret."

She understood what he meant, but she didn't try to pull away. "Let's talk about this, Dillon."

He shook his head. "You see, there's the rub. I don't want to talk."

"But you said you needed someone to talk to."

"I'll find someone else."

"I'm here."

His eyes, so misty gray, so clear, held hers. "This is a bad idea."

Not understanding, but wanting to desperately, she protested. "No, Dillon. We can be friends. We can help each other through this wedding."

"Can we?"

"Yes. I promise. I know it's hard for you, being here again. I'll help you."

"Will you?"

Isabel looked up at him, at his face, so open now, so willing to trust her. She saw hope in the clouds banking in his eyes. "I'll try."

"And what if I try to kiss you again?"

"You wouldn't, would you?"

He touched a finger to her lips. "I want to, right here, right now."

"Dillon—"

"I want to, Issy."

Isabel felt a sigh move through her. A strange humming sound lifted out over the wind, maybe it was her heart beating much too fast. Somehow, she knew, knew that they'd never be able to just talk. There was a sweet, special something here that she'd never felt before with any other man.

"Issy?"

She had her eyes closed. "Hmmm?"

"I'm going to kiss you."

She sighed right along with the pine trees. "Okay."

"Okay, I just wanted to warn you."

"Okay."

Dillon leaned down to pull her close. With one hand pulling through the tangles of her long hair and the other one gentling on the small of her back, he lowered his head to hers. Knowing that he shouldn't be doing it. Knowing that she deserved so much more than he had to offer her. Knowing that they'd both be moving on soon.

Knowing that it felt so right, so pure, so wonderful that he'd never be able to let her go. And while he kissed her, he thanked the God he'd so often fought against for giving him the strength to come home again, to find her here. Even though Dillon hadn't relied on prayer in a long time, he prayed about his feelings for Isabel, and he asked God to release him from all the bad memories. But maybe The Good

Lord didn't want him to forget. Maybe he'd been asking for the wrong things.

It didn't matter right now. Right now, he felt a burst of sheer joy, felt his heart settling down for the first time in a very long time, felt as if he had indeed come home again. Lifting his head, he stared down at her, unable to voice his feelings. Except to say her name. "Isabel."

Isabel watched his face, saw the peaceful expression falling like soft sun rays across his weathered features. "It's going to be all right, Dillon. I promise." Then she lifted up to kiss him again.

For a few minutes, they were lost in each other, there on the edge of the cotton field. Until the roar of an approaching tractor brought them out of their embrace.

And brought Eli Murdock face-to-face with his brother and Isabel Landry.

Eli glared down on them, then cut the engine, leaving a quaking silence to shatter through the trees.

"I told you this was a bad idea," Dillon whispered, all traces of serenity gone from his face now. But he held her hand tightly in his as he turned to face his brother. "I'll handle this."

"No," Isabel said, lifting her head to stare up at Eli. "We'll handle your brother—together."

She didn't miss the pride shining through Dillon's eyes, or the tightening of his fingers around her own.

Eli sat back in his seat, then hopped down from the cab, his harsh features red from heat and disapproval. "I see you two are up to your old tricks."

"Hello, Eli," Isabel said in a level voice, even though her whole body tensed at seeing him again.

She'd avoided him as long as she could. Might as well show him right here and now that she wasn't a scared little girl anymore.

"Isabel," he said by way of greeting. "I mighta known you'd take up with my no-good brother again. Y'all are like two peas in a pod."

Dillon glared at his brother, a steely look cresting in his eyes. "Well, these two peas don't want to be bothered, Eli. What Isabel and I do together is none of your business."

"It is when you're standing on my land," Eli reminded them, his eyes purposely centering on Isabel. "What would Mama think, if she saw you two kissing right here in the middle of the cotton patch."

Dillon let out a long sigh. "First of all, this is my land, too. And I don't think Mama would make a big deal out of this. Isabel and I are adults, after all."

Eli's look of disdain made Isabel feel sick inside. He'd never regard her as anything but poor farm trash. His next words only confirmed that notion.

"Yeah, I can see things have certainly taken a new turn with you two. Used to chase each other around, playing tag and baseball, innocent enough. I reckon you've both grown up, but that doesn't mean you should become careless and irresponsible—with no thought for the consequences."

"Shut up, Eli," Dillon said, the echo of his frustration rising out over the trees. "I won't listen to your insults and I won't let you talk that way about my relationship with Isabel."

Isabel lifted her chin, her gaze meeting Eli's. "It's okay, Dillon." Then to Eli, "You're right, of course. Dillon and I are adults now, and we're also a whole lot older and wiser than we were when we used to run around this place teasing each other and playing games. Don't worry, though, Eli. I wouldn't dream of doing anything to ruin Susan's wedding. And I hope you won't, either."

Turning defensive, Eli said, "And what's that supposed to mean?"

"Take it any way you want," Isabel said, shrugging. "Now, gentlemen, I have to get back to work. Susan wants to see the first shots of her wedding dress. And, in case you've both forgotten, she's having a pantry shower tomorrow night. I'll be taking pictures of that happy occasion, too. So, I'd better get back and finish up today's negatives."

Dillon stood silent, his hand on Isabel's arm. Then he said, "Don't rush off."

"Not on my account anyway," Eli said with a mock smile. Then he added, "Oh, by the way, Isabel, I hear you're making a nice living with that fancy camera of yours. Don't go gouging me for too much money on these wedding pictures. I'd hate to think you'd take advantage of my good graces just 'cause you've gone and got a big head."

Seething, Isabel smiled sweetly at him. "I'm doing this as a favor for Susan and my grandmother," she explained. "And unlike some people, I don't take advantage of others. You can rest assured I'll quote you a fair price for my services, Eli."

Eli nodded, his gaze sweeping her face. "I'll just bet."

A shiver of revulsion slipping down her back, Isabel turned to hurry toward her house, memories of Eli's past innuendoes coming back with all the clarity of the chirping crickets singing to the approaching darkness.

While Dillon had always teased her relentlessly, his youthful flirtations had only fueled her own longings. Eli, on the other hand, had been much older and much more direct with his barbs. He'd always cornered her, making suggestive remarks about her station in life and about her lack of a social position, making her feel small and worthless even while he implied he could give her whatever she wanted—if she'd be willing to pay the price. Isabel had never taken him up on any of his offers. And apparently, he'd never forgiven her for it. Or for her closeness to Dillon.

Isabel tried to block the ugly past and Eli's condescending cruelness out of her mind. But it wouldn't work. Dillon's sweet touch, followed so closely by Eli's implied threats, only reinforced what she'd been telling herself all along.

She should have never returned to Wildwood.

Nothing good could come of this. Especially if she and Dillon didn't halt things between them right now.

Reaching the back porch of the little farmhouse, Isabel turned to stare out into the golden dusk. And then she saw Dillon, moving like a desperado through the wildflowers. Heading toward home.

"Only we don't have a home, do we, Dillon?" she whispered to the night wind. "You and me, we're like that field of flowers, wild and uncultivated, scattered."

And if Eli Murdock had his way, they'd both be mowed down and cleared out.

Chapter Five

"More rice and flour," Cynthia Murdock said, laughing out into the crowd of about twenty women scattered around the opulent formal living room of Eli's home. "Susan, sugar, you'll have to cook rice every night for a year if this keeps up."

Susan laughed, then passed the basket laden with staple provisions around the group, her eyes shining with pleasure. "But isn't this basket so lovely. I can use it in the kitchen maybe, or out on the sun porch." Then, her gaze flying to Cynthia, she hastily added, "That is, if you don't mind me adding my own decorating touches here and there, Mrs. Murdock."

Cynthia took the floral-etched wicker basket filled with not only rice and flour bags, but spices and seasonings, too, then turned to her future daughter-in-law. "Of course not, honey. As far as I'm concerned, when you move in here with my son, my work is done. I plan to fade to the background. I think I'll travel a lot and you know, I might even invest in one of those fancy condominiums down at Panama City Beach. I do so love the Gulf of Mexico.''

"Wish I had an accommodating mother-in-law," one of the shower attendees chirped. "I'd gladly buy mine a condo far away from here, if I could afford it."

Isabel, standing near the high arched doorway to the kitchen, laughed at the offhand joke, then snapped the moment with her camera, her stance aloof and observant as always. She was comfortable being on the outside, looking in. Maybe because she'd been born into that position here at Wildwood, it just came naturally for her now. Perhaps that was why she'd taken up photography at an early age, with an inexpensive camera Grammy Martha had given her one Christmas. Now, she could watch the world from her vantage point and capture the parts of it she wanted to preserve.

Like tonight. Being here in Eli's excessively furnished home only reminded her of being with Dillon in the sparse, ragged remains of Wildwood. Like Dillon, Isabel didn't feel any tuggings toward the new house. No, her heart would always belong to the old mansion across the way.

And her heart was strongly leaning toward the man who'd taken up residence inside that old house. She'd much rather be there, trying to decipher Dillon, than here watching her friend tear open the silver-and-white patterned paper of yet another shower gift. Here amid the belles and matrons of the local society, Isabel felt out of sorts and at odds. She'd never been a part of the inner circle. No, she'd been more of a curiosity for Miss Cynthia's rich friends—someone to patronize and tease. And because of that, she now felt as if she'd been on display all evening.

With comments ranging from, "My, my, it's Isabel Landry, the world traveler. Whatcha doing back in the boonies, sugar?" to "Isabel's gone and got herself citified. I do believe I've never seen shoes like those. And that hair—your poor mama, rest her soul, would take a pair of scissors to that tangle right away, darlin'," she only wanted to finish her pictures and escape the sugary-sweet facade of southern blue-blood wedding shower mania.

"Want a cup of punch, Isabel?" Martha Landry, who'd been hired to help serve, asked from behind her granddaughter. "You look drained."

"Thanks, Grammy." Isabel took the rich red juice concoction laced with a dollop of vanilla ice cream. The creamy mixture felt cool and smooth on her throat. "I am tired. I didn't sleep very well last night."

"I know, honey," Martha said above the din of feminine chatter. "I heard you roaming the house. You used to do that when you were little, remember?"

Isabel smiled, then dipped her head. "Yes, and I'd usually wind up sneaking into your room."

Martha winked. "Grammy's quilts are guaranteed to calm any nighttime fears away. You could still stop in for a visit—you'll never be too old for some comfort."

Tears misted Isabel's eyes. "I might take you up on that offer, Grammy. I'm having a hard time being back here."

Concerned, Martha said, "But your pictures...

Isabel, they're all so pretty. Susan is real pleased so far."

"Then that's worth the trip," Isabel replied, meaning it. "I wouldn't want her to be disappointed, in me or this wedding."

"Don't sound so cynical, dear," Martha whispered. "Just look at the girl. Even if you can't find it in your heart to soften toward Eli, at least be happy for Susan's sake. She's glowing."

"Yes, she is," Isabel said, deciding she wouldn't share the rest of her doubts with her grandmother just yet. "And don't worry, I wouldn't dream of bursting Susan's bubble."

"It's more than a bubble, Isabel," Martha replied, patting her granddaughter's slender arm. "It's a lifelong commitment between two human beings."

"It's downright scary," Isabel admitted, her thoughts automatically slipping to Dillon. "What makes a good marriage, Grammy?"

Martha sighed, then took a sip of her own punch. "Well, that's a loaded question. I guess it's both simple and complicated—it takes love, faith, hope, commitment and compromise. A really good marriage always includes that very important element—the firm belief in God as a guiding force. You know, your parents had all of those things."

"They did adore each other, and they did rely on God's help."

"But?"

Isabel shifted on her chunky sandals. "They just seemed so…resigned. They didn't try to make a better life for themselves. They worked so hard, and for somebody else. I'll never be able to understand that."

Martha's keen eyes scrutinized Isabel's face. "Child, have you ever stopped to consider that your parents had everything they wanted right here?"

Isabel shook her head. "But they could have had so much more. Remember the time Daddy wanted to buy Mama that house in town? They were so excited, so happy. I know they wanted to get away from this place. But nothing ever came of it. It's as if they just gave up on all their dreams."

"Maybe that was more your dream than theirs, sugar," Martha said gently. "You can't misjudge Leonard and Miriam. They had the life they wanted— you see, they had each other."

Seeing the pain and disappointment in her grandmother's eyes, Isabel quickly set her empty punch cup down. "Oh, Grammy, I meant no disrespect. I loved them dearly—you know that. I just didn't always understand them."

Martha put a hand on Isabel's shoulder. "My son was a kind, proud man. A hard worker, like his father. Maybe he was too softhearted, true. He let others dictate to him." Her gaze shifted ever so slightly to Cynthia Murdock. "But he was content with life. He had a strong faith that everything would work out, with The Lord's help."

"You want me to find that kind of faith, don't you?" Isabel said.

"Yes, I surely do," Martha replied in a soft whisper. "And…I want you to find the kind of love your parents had, the kind of relationship I had with your dear grandfather. That, Isabel, is where you'll find your treasures."

Isabel nodded, then looked out the wide window,

over toward the dark shape of Wildwood. "Somewhere out there, I guess I'll find some sort of peace one day."

"Might be closer than you think," Martha said.

Isabel shot her grandmother a look, but Martha was already clapping and admiring the next gift Susan had opened.

Wondering what her grandmother had meant by that pointed observation, Isabel automatically busied herself with taking another picture of Susan. The gift wasn't a kitchen item, however. It was a bath basket, complete with colorful pastel gels and soaps that smelled like a tropical paradise.

"I know it's not officially kitchenware," Beatrice Webster said to her surprised daughter. "But I did get you a food processor. I just couldn't resist throwing this in, too, honey. I got it for your honeymoon—you can take some of the lotions and soaps."

"Oh," Susan said before placing the gift off to the side, her usually bright eyes going flat. "That's so nice of you, Mama." Then to everyone's surprise, at just the moment Isabel snapped another shot of her, Susan blurted out, "There's only one problem. We might not have a honeymoon. Actually, there might not even be a wedding!"

With that, the woman burst into tears and ran to the kitchen, leaving the entire room in a shocked, awkward silence.

"Oh, my," Cynthia said, clearly embarrassed. After all, Murdocks didn't show vulgar displays of emotion in public. Turning to Beatrice, she said, "Maybe I should go and talk to her."

"It's my fault," Beatrice wailed, her face as red as

the ribbon curled around her pudgy fingers. "I shouldn't have sneaked that gift in. I'll go and see what's wrong."

"Let me, Mrs. Webster," Isabel said, stunning not only herself but everyone else in the room. "I mean, it might be better if Susan talks to someone who's not so...involved in all of this."

"Good point," Martha agreed, urging Isabel into the kitchen. "Now, ladies, let's finish these cheese straws. I made them myself and I'll be highly offended if we have any left. And let me see that beautiful tablecloth Irene Stratton sent over—Battenburg lace, isn't it?"

With the even flow of her grandmother's calming voice echoing in her head, Isabel searched the long kitchen for her friend. She found Susan out on the patio, staring into the glistening waters of the kidney-shaped swimming pool.

"Are you all right?" Isabel asked, hesitation making her whisper.

Susan waved a hand, then wiped a couple of fingers under her tear-smudged eyes. "Just prewedding nerves, I guess. I sure made a fool of myself in there, though, didn't I?"

Coming to stand by her friend, Isabel put a hand across Susan's back. The woman was trembling. "Susan, tell me what's going on?"

Near bursting, Susan turned to hug Isabel close, a new batch of sobs racking her body. "It's just...Eli can be so stubborn at times. We had a terrible fight today—he was so moody and mean to me. Something about boll rot or boll weevils—I can't remember which. And now I feel horrible, fighting over some silly bugs!''

Hiding her smile, Isabel hugged her friend tight. ''Oh, Susi, I'll bet he was just worried. I'm sure he didn't mean to take it out on you. But boll weevils can be bad for a cotton crop. And so can boll rot— the crop won't yield as much if the plants can't mature properly.''

Susan let go to stand back and stare at Isabel. ''You think I'm being spoiled and selfish, don't you?''

''No, I think you're a bride—maybe a bit emotional and overstressed, but that's to be expected, I imagine.''

Susan let out a sigh, then plopped down on a wrought-iron bench. ''I never knew such a happy event could cause so many hurt feelings. Eli means well, I know. But…he gets so mad when I suggest even the smallest of changes.''

Wanting to understand, Isabel sat down, too. ''You mean with the wedding?''

''With everything,'' Susan blurted out. ''He doesn't want me to change a thing about this house— not that it needs changing. It's perfect. But that's the problem. I want to add my own touches. You know, make it homey. It seems so lofty and grand, I'm afraid to walk through it for fear of knocking something over and breaking it.''

''I understand,'' Isabel said, looking around at the immaculate yard. ''It needs children running through it and a swing set over there. Little things that make a house a home.''

''Exactly,'' Susan said, bobbing her head. ''And Eli refuses to even discuss children. Plus, he's watched over the plans for the wedding like a general watching over a battle plan. He wants everything to go off without a hitch. 'What would people think if a Murdock had a tacky wedding?' That's exactly what he said to me when I showed him the teal material I'd picked for the bridesmaid dresses. Said it was too loud and bright.''

"I'm sure it was lovely."

Susan hung her head. "No, I have bad taste. I know I do, but Miss Cynthia's helping me there. We settled on a pale pink instead. Oh, Isabel, what if I can never measure up?"

Angry that Eli had inflicted the same kind of pain on Susan as he had her, Isabel jumped up to pace in front of the rippling pool. "That's ridiculous. You more than measure up to Eli Murdock. That man had better tread lightly, or he'll lose the best thing that's ever happened to him."

"I won't leave him at the altar, Isabel," Susan said, her eyes widening. "I truly love him with all my heart, and besides it would devastate him. Not to mention the embarrassment. I'd never be able to hold my head up in Wildwood again."

"Hogwash," Isabel said. "Is that all anybody around here worries about, appearances? If you're having doubts about this wedding, Susan, you'd better halt it now. Before it's too late."

Appalled, Susan jumped up to stop Isabel. "No, I didn't mean to imply that. I fully intend to marry Eli. I love him. I...I just get so confused and worried. And I know he loves me, and he can be incredibly sweet about things. But on days when he's in one of his tempers... Well, I just start doubting if I can ever make him happy."

Isabel didn't want to tell her friend that she seriously doubted anyone could ever make Eli Murdock happy. The man just didn't seem to have any compassion or understanding for his fellow human beings. But she'd already pressed Susan enough, and she knew her interference would only cloud matters.

"Of course you'll make him happy," she told Susan, patting her friend's trembling hand. "You've just got to relax and enjoy being a blushing bride."

Susan still looked dejected. "If he'd only quit being so stubborn—he could hire someone to help oversee things around here. He's trying to run this place with so little help, and it's making him very hard to live with. Not to mention, he never gets to rest. I worry about his health."

"Farming is very demanding work," Isabel said, remembering how hard her father had worked. Rain, drought, wind, fire, pests, a hundred things could go wrong at any given time when you farmed the land. Your livelihood depended on nature and good luck. "Does he have someone reliable who could take over some of the responsibilities?"

"He's got good workers, but..." Susan stopped, her expression guarded and unsure. "Eli says he can't trust anyone else to be in charge. And his mama runs him ragged, demanding his attention."

"Miss Cynthia is a very capable woman herself," Isabel said. "Maybe she could at least take over some of the paperwork."

"But Eli doesn't trust her with any of it," Susan said. "Besides, he doesn't want his mother working."

Giving Isabel another measured look, she said in a shaky voice, "If Dillon would offer a hand—"

"Dillon?" Isabel couldn't help but laugh. "You expect Eli to let Dillon help out on this place, after the way they feel about each other?"

Recovering remarkably, Susan nodded, then sniffed. "Well, I could talk to Eli and you could work on Dillon. I'm sure between the two of us, we could make them see eye to eye on this."

"No," Isabel said, shaking her head as she whirled away. "Dillon doesn't want to get involved in his brother's problems."

"This land isn't a problem," Susan retorted. "This land has been in this family for generations, and the money from this place has helped Dillon through the years. He owes it to his mother and to Eli. He deserted this family. He should be thankful he's even welcome back here at all."

Angry now that Susan had just blurted out all her own problems regarding Wildwood and had just as quickly turned the blame toward Dillon, Isabel said, "I don't know what Eli's told you, Susan. But from what my grandmother's told me, whatever happened between Dillon and Eli all those years ago wasn't all Dillon's fault. Eli, as you're beginning to discover, can be as hardheaded as anyone. And he was always the hardest on Dillon. I just don't think this is a good idea."

"Then I guess I'll just have to handle this the best I can, and hope my groom doesn't call off the wedding." Giving Isabel another pleading look, she said, "At least think about it. If Dillon could stay on a while, that would give Miss Cynthia some time with him, distract her from pestering Eli so much, maybe. And you and Dillon could have some time alone—it's obvious you two are growing close again.''

Hating the logic in Susan's words, and ignoring that last remark, Isabel decided she hadn't given her friend nearly enough credit. Beneath that ditzy persona grew a regular steel magnolia.

''Why, Susan Webster, if I didn't know better I'd think you were deliberately trying to manipulate me.''

Grabbing her arm, Susan said, ''Of course not. I just know that Dillon needs some time here, to reconcile with his mother. And he'd listen to you—you did get him to agree to the tuxedo.'' Lowering her voice, she added, ''And the talk around town is that you two are getting reacquainted in a very big way, if you know what I mean.''

Isabel knew exactly what her friend meant. ''We're friends, good friends. That's all.''

''But Dillon confides in you,'' Susan said on a low whine. ''He's never been civil to anyone around here. He must have some feelings for you.''

''Not really, and that's why I don't want to go another round with him,'' Isabel said, remembering how hard fought the tuxedo victory had been, and how much it had cost her. Many more of Dillon's kisses, and she'd be forever lost here at Wildwood. ''I can't do it, Susan. I won't act as a go-between with Dillon and Eli. Eli's already suspicious enough of my relationship with his brother.''

''Well, you care about Dillon, don't you?''

''Yes, but it's not what you think.''

Her expression hopeful, Susan plowed on.

"Wouldn't you like to give Dillon an opportunity to prove himself? This is the perfect chance for him to get back in Eli's good graces."

"I'm not so sure he needs to prove himself where Eli is concerned. And I won't trick him into doing something he might regret."

"But if you don't at least suggest this to Dillon, you might wind up regretting it yourself," Susan argued. "I just want some time with my new husband, Isabel. I really want to start this marriage off on the right path. Eli needs help, and Dillon's the perfect replacement."

"Dillon hasn't worked this farm in years."

"He's smart. He can figure it all out. Him and his books—he'll get with the program real soon."

"Books? What on earth are you talking about?"

Smiling now, Susan playfully slapped Isabel's arm. "You really are in another world. Dillon owns a chain of bookstores up in Atlanta. That's how he made his money. So he might not be a cotton farmer, but he can sure figure out how to become one. Dillon will just read up on it until he gets it right. That's how he always does things." Clearly recovered now, Susan turned. "I'm going back in. I feel better already. I'll explain to everyone that Eli and I had a little spat and I was feeling sorry for myself."

Pivoting, she said, "Think about this, Isabel. And talk to Dillon, please. He'll listen to you."

"Okay, I'll think about it." Right now, however, she was more surprised about Dillon's new life, than Eli's bad attitude.

Watching in amazement as Susan pranced back inside, Isabel let out a low sigh. So Dillon's business venture happened to be a bookstore or two?

Books. The man had never once mentioned anything about being bookish. He'd said he owned his own business, but she'd never dreamed it was a bookstore. Oh, it was just like Dillon to let her jump to conclusions and assume that he was still as wild and unsettled as he'd been as a youth. He never was any good at defending himself or talking about himself.

Maybe because he knew everyone would automatically think the worst, just as she had. What if Susan had a point? What if Dillon could use this opportunity to end this bitterness with his brother. Eli could certainly use the help and support, and his mother would be thrilled to have her family back together.

"No, I won't talk to him." But even as she denied it, Isabel looked toward the dark mansion. "No, I can't get involved in this." She was about to turn away, when a light flickered on in the back of the house, in the kitchen.

A single candle burning in the darkness like a beacon. A beckoning glow, reaching out to her in the night.

Telling herself she was crazy, she followed that light.

Maybe it wouldn't hurt just to see how he felt about helping out around here—just for a couple of weeks.

After all, all he could say was no.

Chapter Six

"**No.**"

Dillon said the one word into the cellular phone nestled at his ear, his eyes scanning the screen of the laptop computer blinking in front of him. "I don't care if we will lose money or momentum. I don't intend to compromise on quality, Sanford. If the quality isn't there, then we don't expand right now. All five stores are holding steady, especially the original on Peachtree. We'll survive until next year without expanding into the Carolinas just yet."

Clicking the small phone shut, Dillon sat staring out into the summer night. The lullaby of singing crickets mingled with the strands of a warm, soft wind flowing through the open windows in front of him. His business manager and lawyer, Sanford Reynolds, wasn't too happy with him right now. Sanford had advised more expansion, but Dillon wasn't quite ready to tackle everything that went into building and opening another store.

Not now. Not when he was back here at Wildwood and he had a million scattered emotions blinking through his mind like fireflies. Rhyme and Reason, as his chain of eclectic bookstore-coffeehouses, was aptly called, would just have to wait.

He needed a little rhyme and reason of his own right now. He needed to stop thinking about Isabel Landry.

Remembering yesterday, remembering kissing her there in that field, Dillon let the darkness shroud his doubts while he remembered the feel of her in his arms.

But the ugly vision of his brother staring down on them with condemning wrath quickly broke through the sweetness of that particular daydream. Eli would cause trouble for them, just as he always had. Dillon could handle it; he'd learned to let his brother's taunts and disapproval roll right off his back—or at least he'd learned to avoid Eli by staying away. But he wouldn't allow Eli to inflict any more pain on Isabel. Yesterday's encounter in the cotton patch had only reinforced the uneasy feeling Dillon always had around his older brother. Things had gone from bad to worse after Isabel had left them.

"I can't believe you're taking up with her again," Eli had said, contempt clear in each word.

"That's none of your concern, brother," Dillon had retorted. "Anyway, why do you care? You're engaged, remember? You're about to be married. I don't think your lovely bride would appreciate the way you stare at Isabel Landry."

And Dillon certainly didn't appreciate it. It made him sick—just as it always had. Eli might be attracted to Isabel, but she would never, ever be good enough in Eli's eyes to take the attraction any further.

But Eli was obviously still in denial where Isabel was concerned. "I don't know what you're talking about."

Dillon inched closer to his brother. "Oh, yes, you do. We both know what I'm talking about. I walked away from you once, Eli, to protect Isabel and her family. And I've regretted it ever since. You might not get so lucky this time."

"Are you threatening me, little brother?"

"No, I'm telling you that I want you to stay away from Isabel. She's done nothing to you. She never did. You just can't seem to tolerate anyone who doesn't have blood as blue as yours. So stop playing your cruel games and concentrate on your marriage."

"While you concentrate on that low-class woman who's sponged off us all her life?"

Dillon's whole body had tensed; he came close to hitting his brother. And the dare in Eli's eyes only fueled that need. But, sanity and practiced self-control kicked in as Dillon remembered all the other times his brother had set him off, then had blamed him for the whole thing. This time, it would be different. This time, he'd stay in control. Instead of doing what Eli expected him to do, he'd pushed past Eli, determined to keep a civil tongue for his mother's sake.

Then he'd turned, pointing a finger at his brother. "Isabel Landry has more class in her pinkie than you'll ever have your whole life, brother. And you know as well as I do that Isabel never took advantage of living here. Good grief, Eli, they lived in a shack. They barely made ends meet."

"That so-called shack was rent-free," Eli had reminded him with self-righteous disdain. "And they lived off this land, had plenty of fresh meat and vegetables. And still Isabel walked around like she ought to be a queen or something. Now, she's even worse. I didn't want her here for the wedding, but Mama and Susan insisted. That girl thinks she can flaunt it over us now that she's been away from here for a while if you ask me."

"I didn't ask you," Dillon replied, disgusted that his own brother could have such an attitude about someone who'd never done a thing to him. But that didn't matter to Eli. His narrow-minded snobbery was very intact, and buried so deep Dillon doubted his brother would ever change.

Because Isabel was a distraction, because Eli was as attracted to her as Dillon had always been, his older brother had taken out his frustrations on her. He didn't want to like Isabel, didn't want to feel anything for her, so he turned his feelings into intolerance, lashing out at the very source of his woes.

And he'd lash out again, if Dillon didn't stop him. Torn between wanting to get reacquainted with Isabel, and the need to protect her from Eli's rash behavior, Dillon wondered if he'd be able to control his own yearnings. It wasn't fair to Isabel, when he knew he couldn't stay here much longer.

His thoughts coming back to the blinking cursor of his latest sales report, Dillon reminded himself he only had a few more days here. He took a long, heaving breath, focusing on something serene—the green of Isabel's eyes maybe, but the thought of looking into her wild, forest-rich eyes only agitated him more.

Then he stretched back in the rickety old desk chair he'd dragged to the table by the window. He could do this. He could attend his brother's wedding, be civil, then get away from here all in one piece.

That is, if he could just stop thinking about Isabel.

Thinking about her conversation with Susan, Isabel walked the worn clay path through the iridescent wildflowers, moonlight guiding her to the back steps of the old plantation house. She shouldn't be here. She should stick to her plan of doing her job and nothing else. Despite Susan's pleas, Isabel had not wanted to get involved with the Murdock brothers again.

But here she stood—yet again.

When she heard the sad, beautiful sound of Spanish guitar music coming from a radio, she closed her eyes and listened to the soothing melody. Maybe now would be a good time to lift up a prayer for guidance. She could sure use some. So she stood there for a moment, silent and waiting, while the music and the night soothed her worries to a slow simmering.

Through the long kitchen windows she saw Dillon sitting at a desk, a lamp burning brightly at his side, the window nearest him thrown open to the night. Well, he must have ordered the electricity to be turned on, at least. Curious, she inched up on the porch to get a better look. And was surprised to find him hard at work with a laptop in front of him there on the table.

Dillon, working at a computer! Another myth shattered. She wouldn't have believed he even knew how to turn one on. No, cars and motorcycles were more his mode of operation. Fast cars. Fast motorcycles. Like the one parked out in the tractor shed, sleek and black and loaded with chrome. And classical guitar? She had Dillon pegged for loud rock and roll.

Bookish? Did a man who drove such a machine really read books and listen to classical music?

Apparently, in the ten years that he'd been away, Dillon had made some sort of peace with himself. He'd obviously gained a certain strength from what he knew to be true in his heart. She wondered, though, if being back here might shatter that peace and test that strength. Shaking her head, she supposed it was possible she had misjudged Dillon. After all, there had always been a side to him that he'd kept hidden from the world. Even her.

High time she found out about that side.

She stepped up on a creaky plank, then stopped. This could be dangerous. She was already infatuated with Dillon, always had been. Maybe it would be best if she just left things the way they were. She didn't want him to endear himself to her anymore, and seeing this side of him—this gentle side of the boy she'd always remembered—might make her long for things she could never have.

She turned to leave.

The back door swung open. "Spying on me, Issy?"

Too late to run away now.

She did a hesitant twirl, smiled up at him, then sucked in the breath that rushed out of her body at the sight of him in jeans and a loose, half-buttoned shirt, his dark hair spiked across his forehead. "Yeah, you caught me. But I guess that's the only way I'm ever gonna find out about what makes you tick, Dillon.''

His dark eyes reflected the pale gray of the moon's light. "That curious, huh?"

"I...I heard your music," she hedged. "I was intrigued."

"Intrigued?" He chuckled, then reached a hand out to her. "There's nothing intriguing about me, honey. Just trying to get through another day."

Easing up onto the porch, she stared at him, the touch of his fingers on her hand a reminder of how he made her feel inside. "Why didn't you tell me?"

His chin lifted a notch. "Tell you what?"

"That you like to read? That you're...how did Susan put it...bookish?"

He dropped her hand. "Susan chatters too much."

"What do you do for a living, Dillon?"

"Didn't Susan tell you all about that, too?"

"She said you own a chain of bookstores. I thought I'd heard her wrong."

Her doubt, so honest, so straightforward, stung Dillon like a wasp. He was so very tired of trying to prove himself. "I get by."

"Then it's true?"

"Don't sound so shocked," he said, mimicking her very words when he'd told her she was pretty.

Realizing he was on the defensive, Isabel changed her tactic. "I'm not shocked. I'm impressed. Very. If I recall correctly, you had a certain disdain for any and all books in high school. Never studied, never even opened a textbook."

"I passed, didn't I?"

"Yes, you did." She'd forgotten that his grades

were always just about as good as her own. And she'd
had to study for hours on end. But Dillon—he'd never
seemed too worried.

Then, she'd chalked it up to irresponsibility.

Now, she wasn't so sure. About anything. Except
the dark light in his eyes and the way his fingers
stroked her skin as he stood there daring her to doubt
him.

"I'm sorry," she said finally. "I guess I didn't really know you after all." Pulling away, she added,
"And I guess you don't really *want* me to know you,
after all."

He tugged her back. "Yes, I do. More than you
can possibly imagine."

She was imagining lots of things right now. "Then
talk to me, Dillon."

"I told you—I don't want to talk."

With that, he pulled her into his arms and kissed
her without self-defense or self-doubt. Then he let her
go, his breath like a warm wind moving over her hair.
"I could hurt you, Isabel. And I won't risk that."

"I'm a big girl," she managed to whisper.
"And…I've survived being hurt before."

"I won't hurt you again," he said, each word a
declaration.

Something in his tone told her that he knew her
deepest, darkest secret. Dillon knew that she'd always
cared about him. And now, he was deliberately trying
to warn her away, because he couldn't return her feelings.

"I'd better go," she said, needing to distance herself from his touch, and from the truth.

Susan would just have to find some other way to

help Eli. Isabel wasn't about to ask Dillon for anything. Not when she felt so raw and in pain that even the humid summer wind on her back felt like bramble moving across her skin.

"Yes," Dillon said, the one word heavy with regret. "You'd better go. And you'd better stay away. I'm no good for you, Isabel. No good."

Dazed, she said, "Maybe it's still the other way around. Maybe I'm no good for you."

She'd walked down the steps, when she heard him call out to her. "Isabel, do you think...do you think God listens to Spanish guitar music when He's feeling lonely?"

Isabel stopped, her back to him, her gaze lifting up to the stars. Oh, how she wanted to be immune to that sweet pain she heard in his words. "I'm sure He does, Dillon." Then she turned to face him. "And, He listens to lonely people, too. If you won't talk to me, then I know in my heart you can talk to God."

She turned, and though she couldn't see his face, Isabel knew Dillon's eyes were on her.

"I don't think God will want to listen to a loser like me," he said.

"God doesn't see us as losers, Dillon. You know that. God sees us as His children. And He's always willing to listen."

"I've tried to talk to Him, really I have. I've tried to pray about things—about coming home. We just never know when it's really right, do we?"

"We have to trust in Him, or so Grammy tells me."

"So you have doubts, too?"

"I do, sometimes." She glanced around at the

beautiful night, then back at the silhouette of the man in front of her. "But when I look up at the stars or see these beautiful flowers that keep coming back here year after year, I know that God is watching over us. It's up to us to let Him take control, Dillon."

Dillon was silent for a minute, then he said, "Do you think God's watching over Wildwood?"

"Always," she said without hesitation. "Can't you see Him here, Dillon? Can't you feel Him in the wildflowers, in the oak trees, out in the wind in the fields? He's here."

"I wonder why He brought me back here," Dillon said."

"Because it's home," Isabel answered, more to herself than to Dillon. "We're both home for a reason."

"And it has nothing to do with Eli's fancy wedding, does it?"

"I can't answer that," she replied softly, her hands wrapped against her chest, her head down as she stared at the dirt and the soft, ethereal glow of flowers all around her.

"I know," he said into the night. "Now, go home and get some rest. The rehearsal supper is in a few days."

"Will you be there?"

Dillon hesitated, thought about his need to be near her, thought about his brother's need to be cruel. Maybe he should be there, just to watch over Isabel. Telling himself he shouldn't do this, he asked her, "Will you sit by me when you're not snapping pictures?"

"Should I, after you just warned me away not five minutes ago?"

"Probably not, but you don't seem the type to heed warnings, anyway."

"I'm not afraid of you, Dillon. I'd like to get to know you—the real you. So will you come to the rehearsal dinner?"

"Will you sit by me and make sure I behave?"

Smiling, she remembered they'd had this conversation before. "All right, I'll sit by you, if you *promise* to behave."

"Then I'll be there. I'm not the best man, of course. But I get to be an usher, at least."

"I'm proud of you—for doing this for your mother."

"Are you, really?"

Repeating his earlier words, she said, "More than you can ever imagine, Dillon."

Silence, then a shifting of feet. "Good night, Issy."

"Good night, Dilly."

Then, "I do own a chain of bookstores. And I do love to read. Come on back some night and I'll pull out a volume of Keats or Shelley and I'll read poems to you by the light of a single candle."

Touched by that gentle image, she said, "A romantic, too? Dillon, you are full of surprises."

"Yeah, that's me."

With that, he was gone. She heard the soft thud of the screen door, then watched as the lamp went out.

Turning, Isabel was left with only the moon to guide her home. The way looked long and empty and lonely.

* * *

The rehearsal dinner was being held at the Camellia Country Club, an exclusive golf and tennis retreat for the few in the area who could afford the monthly membership fees.

Isabel had never been invited to any of the social events at the club, but she'd often heard stories about the tradition and beauty of the place from Susan and her other school friends who had been part of the more popular crowd.

Tonight, Isabel stood on the stone steps leading up to the glass doors of the banquet room, wondering how she would be received now. It was funny, really, that the very people who'd shunned her when she was growing up poor on Wildwood, now welcomed her back with open arms and glowing praise. Funny how a little fame and fortune could turn people's opinions around.

Once, Isabel would have relished being a part of Wildwood society. Now, she only wanted to run away from the glare of its too harsh light. Because, she knew in her heart, they were curious simply because she had seemed so hopeless to them before. It was a morbid curiosity, not a friendly one. They wondered how she'd done it. How had the poor, odd farm girl succeeded against so many obstacles? And, she believed, they somehow envied her even while they regarded her with a quiet disdain.

Well, I survived all of you, she told herself now as she stared up into the chandelier-adorned entrance, her hands sweaty and her breath coming too fast. *I went out and made it, in spite of your low opinions of me.* Her victory, however, was hollow. She would never really triumph over this small-town mentality until she could learn to accept and forgive it. But she would go in there and do her job.

"You were the prettiest girl at the church," a deep male voice said from behind her.

Whirling, she saw Dillon standing by a potted cedar tree, his eyes bright with amusement and questions. "I mean it, Isabel. You far outshone the nervous bride and her stand-in, and any of the fifty or so bridesmaids. I like your dress."

Nervous herself, Isabel smoothed the floral cotton of her sleeveless fitted sheath, then patted the upswept coil of hair centered on top of her head. "Thank you, but there's only about seven bridesmaids in all."

"Looked like at least fifty to me," Dillon commented as he sauntered up the steps. His tie was crooked, and so was his smile. "Of course, I stopped counting once you started flashing that camera. It was more fun to watch you. You really enjoy your work, don't you?"

"Yes, I do," she admitted as he came to stand on the same step with her. "I got a few shots of you, you know."

"Give me the negatives," he said briskly, while his eyes teased her. "Can't have any evidence lying around."

"Evidence that you did indeed show up?"

"Yeah, something like that." Then he leaned close. "How'd I do, anyway?"

"You were the best usher I've ever seen." And the best-looking one. Dillon filled out his casual sports coat and khaki pants rather nicely.

"No, I mean, how did I act?" he asked, his eyes on her.

"You were a perfect gentleman, but do you really care?"

"I care about your opinion of me. And I did see my mother beaming a time or two."

"She was proud of both her sons tonight."

Dillon nodded, looked around, then took her arm under his. "Now, on to the celebration. I think I can manage this if you stick with me. I'll be the envy of every other usher in the place."

"So, you're using me for your own purposes?"

"Haven't I always?" The teasing light went out of his eyes then. He stopped her as they entered the carpeted lobby. "Isabel, I hope you know that I'd never use you. You...you mean a lot to me. Seeing you again has meant a lot to me."

There was a *but* in there somewhere. You mean a lot to me, but...we can't be together. We have to remain just as we always were, secret cohorts. We can't take it any further than that.

It would be so hard, but she'd have to honor his silent conviction. Because it was the only thing she could do.

Touched, she said, "Me, too, Dillon. I'm glad you're my usher tonight."

He leaned close again. "Let's get this show on the road, then we'll sneak out and go back to Wildwood."

"Sounds good."

They both looked up to find Eli staring at them across the expanse of the lobby, his brown eyes flashing disgust and disapproval.

"Get a shot of that," Dillon said, then winked at her as if to ease her concerns.

Isabel didn't miss the uneasiness in his words, though. Nor did she miss the unbridled hostility between the two brothers as they passed each other.

Eli gave them a plastic smile. "Mother wanted you both here tonight," he reminded them, his features set in a serene line for any passersby. "But I expect you both to be on your best behavior. I won't have either of you making a scene at this dinner."

"You mean like this?" Dillon said just before he pulled Isabel close and gave her a quick kiss on the cheek.

Pulling away, Isabel shot a warning look at Dillon, then turned to Eli. "Relax, Eli. Dillon and I are just friends. Nothing more."

"Yeah, she's right," Dillon said, regret evident in his words. "Nothing more, brother. And certainly, nothing less."

Chapter Seven

"Nothing less than the best for my bride," Eli announced to the people gathered in the private dining room at the Camellia Country Club. Amid the clatter of crystal and the sighs of those surrounding him at the elaborately decorated table, he raised Susan's hand and kissed it. "Here's to you, Susan."

Everyone applauded the happy couple then settled in to enjoy the dinner of prime rib and all the trimmings. Susan beamed, her eyes bright and shining, her sighs filled with dreams and hopes, her hand touching on her future husband's sleeve now and again.

"Kinda sickening, don't you think?" Dillon whispered close to Isabel's ear. "My brother can really lay it on thick when he needs to. Does the word *hypocrite* come to mind?"

"Don't sound so cynical," Isabel whispered back. "Even if you and I aren't the marrying kind, you have to admit Eli seems to genuinely love Susan."

Dillon shrugged, wondering where she'd gotten the impression that he wasn't the marrying kind, then speared a cut of the juicy meat centered on his gold-rimmed dinner plate. "Yeah, he loves her all right. Like he loves his hunting trophies and his Peanut Farmer of the Year award. Susan's another conquest to add to his many accomplishments."

Surprised at the venom in his words, Isabel dropped her fork to stare over at him. "Why do you and your brother hate each other so much?"

Dillon leaned back on the mauve brocade chair. "Just your basic sibling rivalry, darlin'."

"It's more than that, and you know it. I remember you fighting when we were growing up, but this goes deeper. What happened between you two, Dillon?"

He glanced over at her, his eyes going into that deep gray zone that she knew meant he didn't intend to answer her question. Except with a question. "What happened to celebrating this blessed occasion?"

Determination clouding her better judgment, Isabel leaned close. "Oh, no, that trick won't work tonight. I want some answers."

"And I want you to smile for me," he countered, his expression guarded and cautious. "If I wanted to talk about my troubles with big brother, I certainly wouldn't do it here, tonight."

He had a point there. She sat back in her own chair and glared down at the remains of her baked potato and marinated asparagus spears. She was just about to tell him they'd discuss this later when Susan motioned to her from the doorway of the room.

"Want to come with me to powder my nose, Isabel?"

"Sure." Seeing the desperation and determination in the other woman's eyes, Isabel couldn't refuse. Turning to Dillon, she said, "I'm going to the ladies' room. Hold my spot."

"Of course." Dillon glanced up in time to see Susan's worried expression. "Don't tell me the bride's getting cold feet?"

"Just a case of the jitters," Isabel assured him. "She probably wants me to get some more shots of the dinner crowd."

"Well, tell her you're off duty now."

"I'll be right back," she assured him, wishing she could feel confident about Susan's intentions. She had a sneaking feeling Susan was going to press her about getting Dillon to stay and help with the crops.

And she was right.

"Have you talked to him?" Susan asked the minute they entered the vanity area of the elegant powder room.

"No," Isabel replied firmly, glaring at her friend in the gilted mirror's reflection. "Susan, I can't do this. I can't ask Dillon to stay here—he's only here tonight because of his mother."

"Well, isn't that just great. Doesn't he even care that Eli's working his fingers to the bone to try to save Wildwood?"

Alarmed at Susan's exaggerations, Isabel turned to face the other woman. "Don't be so dramatic, Susan. Wildwood seems to be thriving. You just need more attention from Eli."

Gripping Isabel's arm, Susan shook her head, causing her golden curls to spill around her face. "No, I'm not being selfish, Isabel. Eli needs to find some help before this place kills him."

"What's going on?" Isabel asked, real concern filtering through her resistance. Susan looked so panicked, so afraid, that Isabel knew this was about more than wedding jitters.

Falling across the mint green velvet divan centered in the small lounge, Susan glanced around to make sure they were alone. "It's Wildwood. Eli's trying so hard to hang on, Isabel. But…things aren't so good."

Shocked, Isabel bent down in front of Susan. "Tell me."

Susan lowered her head, then whispered, "Well, Eli hasn't come out and told me anything, but I've figured it out for myself. I think he's heavily in debt…what with the house and this huge investment in getting this cotton crop going. He's overextended himself a bit and now he's worried sick about it. That's why he's been so moody lately." Grabbing Isabel's hands, she looked up, her eyes wide with fear. "I don't care about the wedding. I just want Eli to be happy. I want to make him happy, but if he loses Wildwood—"

"This can't be happening," Isabel said. "Wildwood has always been so secure, so formidable. What about all the money Mr. Murdock left to the family?"

Susan wiped a hand under her eyes. "Apparently, there wasn't a whole lot of that after Mr. Murdock died. And with Dillon taking every penny his mother could give him and leaving Eli to take care of things—well, maybe now you can understand why I think he needs to help his brother out."

Isabel sank down on the divan beside her trembling friend. "You're right. This is much worse than I imagined. I'm surprised Eli's even coherent enough to go through with the wedding. I'm sure he's worried sick."

"He is," Susan said, tears springing to her eyes. "I've told him over and over I'll call the whole thing off. We could have something simple and less expensive, but he insists that we're going to keep up appearances. And besides, my folks are paying for most of it, anyway."

"Appearances!" Isabel sprang up to pace the length of the narrow sitting area. "Now, that's a Wildwood tradition, if I ever heard one. Appearances mean everything. Mustn't let people know the truth, no matter the cost. How antiquated and futile, Susan. That old southern pride kicks in every time, though."

Susan stood, too, worry causing tiny wrinkles to appear between her carefully plucked eyebrows. "You can't say anything to Eli, Isabel. But you've got to explain this situation to Dillon. Let him offer to stay and help, that's all. Make it look like a peace offering."

"Just to keep Eli's pride and ego intact! Susan, that would be like sending Dillon to the slaughter. He'd have to bow down to his brother all over again. I can't do it."

"Do what?" Cynthia Murdock said from the doorway. "My goodness, girls, this is a celebration, remember. Why do you two look as if someone just died or something?"

"She doesn't have a clue," Susan whispered

through stiffly clenched teeth, then turned with a bubbling smile toward her mother-in-law.

"We were just discussing last minute details, Mrs. Murdock," Isabel said, hating all of this deception. "I was trying to convince your stubborn future daughter-in-law that I don't think I can pull off the shot she's requesting."

"Oh, we'll work on such stuff later," Cynthia admonished, waving jeweled fingers in the air. "Right now, I want you both back in the dining room. I have a special surprise." Smiling like a conspirator, she said, "I'm going to officially welcome Dillon back into the fold—publicly—so there will be no mistake that I'm glad to have my son home."

Isabel's eyes widened as she watched Susan's strained features. Tonight wouldn't be a good time to try to bring her sons together, but Cynthia looked very determined.

"Do something," Susan mouthed while Cynthia checked her hair and makeup in the mirror.

Isabel didn't have time to wonder what she was supposed to do. Cynthia, pleased with her bright red lipstick, ushered them out into the lobby.

"Come along, children," she said, her cream pumps clicking on the marble floorway. "Everyone is waiting."

"What took so long?" Dillon asked when Isabel sank back down into her chair. "You missed dessert—I ate your lemon pie."

"I couldn't eat another bite," Isabel said in what she hoped was a controlled tone, wondering how in the world she could possibly stop Cynthia Murdock from inadvertently causing further hostility between Dillon and Eli.

"You don't look too hot," Dillon said, his eyes flashing between concern and cynicism. "Are you all right? Did Susan say something to upset you?"

Isabel's chuckle was shaky. She supposed she could bring a halt to the proceedings in the old-fashioned way—she could faint. But that wasn't her style. No, best to just let the evening take its course, then get Dillon out of here as soon as possible.

"I'm okay. I just got a little warm—it's so stuffy with the humidity outside. Maybe we could leave early—it looks like rain."

"That wouldn't do for Eli's cotton crop at this stage," Dillon said dryly, missing her request to leave. "Boll rot." Then, "Here, drink some water."

Isabel took a big gulp of the sparkling water with lemon. It felt good going down, and calmed her nerves to a more rational state. Dillon's attention had certainly perked up at the mention of rain. Maybe he was more worried about his brother's doings than he was letting on. "Do you know a whole lot about growing cotton?"

"I know a whole lot about farming," he countered. "Remember, I grew up on a farm."

"I remember," she replied, thinking this could be a good time to suggest that he might want to stick around and help his brother. "It's just that you never seemed as dedicated as Eli."

Dillon's features sharpened into the scowl she remembered so well. "I loved Wildwood," he said simply. "Loved the smell of the wet peanuts after a spring rain, loved the feel of corn silk rushing through my hands. Sorry, I'm getting a bit too poetic on you, Isabel, but I always loved farming. It's just that with Eli hovering over me, I didn't get to put any of my theories into practice."

"Theories?" She stared at him as realization hit her. Dillon was a thinker. He stood quietly and listened, really listened, to the world around him. Yes, he probably did know everything there was to know about farming. And, he was probably chomping at the bit to be included in his brother's new venture. Maybe Susan had a point after all. Maybe. But if she didn't try to get Dillon out of here soon, it wouldn't matter.

"Dillon—"

"I'd like to thank everyone for coming tonight," Cynthia said just then, standing at the head of the table, her smile wide. "I'm so proud of my sons— both my sons—and since this is a celebration, I have a special announcement tonight."

Eli glanced over at Susan, his dark eyes immediately questioning. Isabel figured he didn't like surprises; Eli liked to be in control at all times, nothing was supposed to escape his attention or his approval. Susan's smile was a strained line against her pale face, but she gave a valiant effort at comforting her fiancé by patting his hand and kissing him chastely on the cheek.

Dillon shrugged and quirked a brow toward Isabel. "Mother's always up to something, isn't she?"

"She loves her family," Isabel said by way of a warning.

Cynthia's soft gaze moved from Eli's frowning face to Dillon's puzzled one. "Tonight, I'd like to officially welcome my younger son, Dillon, back to

Wildwood. We've missed you, son, and we just want you to know that you will always have a home with us.'' With that, Cynthia came around the table and stopped at Dillon's chair, then leaned down to hug her son close.

Surprised and clearly uncomfortable at being thrust into the spotlight, Dillon stood to return his mother's affection. ''I love you, Mother,'' he said, his voice low. ''Thank you.''

Cynthia let go of her son, but held a hand on his arm. Then she looked down the table at Eli. ''Son, won't you join me in welcoming your brother home?''

Isabel held her breath as she watched the play of expressions moving over Eli's harsh features. He stood, shock and anger evident in his every move. Throwing down his white linen napkin, Eli stalked around the table to confront his stunned mother.

''So, we kill the fatted calf for my brother? Is that it, Mother? We welcome him back with open arms and no questions asked, after the way he abandoned us, after the way he squandered Daddy's hard-earned money?'' Glaring at Dillon, Eli extended a hand, but the gesture was anything but brotherly or forgiving. ''Welcome home, brother. Did you run out of money? Did your fancy bookstore go under? Is that why you came back to Wildwood?''

A hiss of embarrassed shock rushed through the hot, crowded room, followed by a rush of sandpaper sharp whispers. Dillon didn't reach for his brother's hand. He just stood there, his features etched in granite, the pulse at his jaw vibrating a pounding beat as blood rushed to his face.

Clearly appalled, Cynthia grabbed Eli's arm. "Son, please. You have to let go of all of this bitterness. It's time you forgive your brother and remember that he is family."

Eli jerked his arm away. "I can't do that, Mother. Not now, not tonight. You can forgive Dillon if you want, but I can't."

With that, he turned and motioned for Susan. She rushed to his side, her eyes bright with unshed tears, her head down. But before Eli could take his intended and leave, Dillon sent his chair crashing across the soft carpet as he pushed away from the table.

"Stay, brother, and celebrate your wedding. I'll go and you can pretend I was never here. That's what you've been doing for years now." Then he turned to his mother. "I'm sorry."

With that, he pivoted and stalked out of the room, his back straight and his head high. Only Isabel had seen the gleam of tears forming in his stormy eyes.

And only Isabel knew the hurt he was feeling right now.

Which is why she got up and ran after him.

"Dillon, wait," Isabel called as she followed him out into the parking lot. Off in the distance, thunder warned of an impending storm.

"I don't think so," he said over his shoulder. Then he reached his motorcycle and slung one leg over the padded leather seat. "I've had enough celebrating for one night, Issy."

"Then I'm coming with you," she said, throwing her leg over the seat behind him. Quickly pulling her skirt down, she slung her camera bag across her shoulder and held on to his waist. "Let's go."

"Go home," he said. "You don't need to baby me, Isabel. And you certainly don't need to be seen with me."

"I'm not babying you," she snapped at his neck. "And since when does it matter who I'm seen with around here? I don't want to stay in there—they're wrong about you, Dillon."

That statement brought his head around. "What makes you think that, sugar?"

Looking up at him, then down at the dark concrete, she shook her head. "I don't know. Or maybe I do know. I know you, Dillon. And until you tell me everything, I'm just going to have to go on my instincts and faith."

"Faith?" His laugh sounded more like a snarl. "You know, I was beginning to have some faith, until tonight. Now I'm not so sure."

"Just drive," Isabel replied, her hands clutching his waist. "Just drive, Dillon."

He did, fast and as far away from the bright gleam of the country club's deceptively welcoming haze as he could get. Past the city limit sign out on the county line road, past the rolling farmland and the creekbeds and the rows of pecan trees, past the fields of Wildwood Plantation. Dillon didn't stop the Harley until there was nothing but night and stars left in the world.

Night and stars and Isabel.

She'd come with him. She'd believed in him. Maybe God had heard some of his prayers after all.

Finally, he pulled the snarling machine off the side of the road and down a dirt lane that led past cotton and cornfields to a big pond on the far back side of Wildwood property. His father used to bring Eli and him fishing here. But he refused to think about that tonight.

Instead, he turned to Isabel and lifted her off the long seat, then stood her there in front of him, his hands never leaving the small of her back.

Isabel heaved a deep, calming breath. "That was some ride."

His wild eyes roamed her face. "Did I scare you?"

"No, not really. I was more scared for your emotional state than any physical danger."

"I'm fine, sweetheart. After all, I'm used to being the black sheep of the Murdock family."

"You're not a black sheep, Dillon."

"And how can you be so sure?"

She tossed her heavy camera bag on the bike's seat, then put a hand to his face. "Because, I know you. I've always known you. But, I have to be honest— you had me going there for a while. You played your part so well."

"And what part is that? The bad son, the one who brought ruination to the entire clan?"

"Something like that. You've just let people believe what they wanted to believe, haven't you? Why haven't you ever defended yourself, Dillon?"

He stared down at her, wondering how she could see into his very soul. Wondering why her words hurt even while they brought a tremendous relief. Finally, he said, "I got tired of defending myself."

"So, you just gave up?"

He wasn't ready to tell her everything; to tell her that he'd witnessed such hatred and such venom in his brother's heated words all those years ago, that he didn't think he'd ever be able to forget it. And he wasn't ready to tell her all the reasons he'd left like the coward he was. So instead, he told her, "Yes. I gave up. My brother will never...love me, Issy."

The catch in his words tore through her. Wasn't that what everyone wanted, deep down inside, to be loved, to be accepted?

She certainly knew how he felt. "Why can't he love you, Dillon?"

Dillon shifted, brought her closer. "I don't know for certain. But I think it has something to do with Eli's paranoia about my father." He hesitated a moment, then continued. "Eli always thought I was my father's favorite."

Isabel remembered Roy Murdock very well. Remembered his stern, no-nonsense countenance, his my-way or no-way attitude, the unrelenting grip he had held over his sons and the whole town. And she also remembered his soft spot—Dillon. In spite of his gruff exterior, Roy had always helped Dillon through the worst of escapades.

"Well, you were his favorite. Everybody thought that because of the way he protected you and spoiled you."

Dillon laughed harshly. "That's because my father played his part well, too. He got me out of jams and stood up for me to keep the family name intact. But he always let me know my shortcomings when we were alone. And my poor mother never went against his word, except to send me money here and there."

Surprised, Isabel asked him, "You mean, your father wasn't just spoiling you, the way everyone thought?''

''No, he was inflicting his authority, flexing his power. Eli tried to be the golden boy, the one who could do no wrong. Always there, working hard, trying to make our parents proud.''

''And you, you did everything you could to be a rebel?''

''Yeah, that was me. That's the Dillon they all remember so well.''

Isabel was beginning to understand and see the pattern. Eli, so proud, so conscientious, so willing to please. And Dillon, not really caring, not really trying. And yet, the Murdocks kept forgiving him, kept giving him one more chance. Just as the Bible told them to do, or just to save face? Maybe Eli hated his brother because of that.

''He can't forgive you, because your parents always did, or so it seemed,'' she said, the words coming out in a whisper. ''So much bitterness, such a long time to hold a grudge.''

Dillon moved away from her then, turning in the moonlight to stare out into the black waters of the rippling pond. ''And I deserve every bit of it. I deserve everything Eli throws at me and more.''

She touched a hand to his arm, forced him around. ''What makes you say that?''

Dillon held her by her shoulders. He had to make her understand why he kept fighting against her. ''He's right, Issy. I deserted him. I left them—all of them. I wasn't even here when my father died. Didn't even come home for the funeral.''

She believed there was good in him. She'd seen

that good in the dark corners of his beautiful, sad eyes. "I'm sure you wanted to be here, Dillon."

"You're so sure about me, huh? So sure. My beautiful Isabel. You could almost make me believe in myself again, the way you cling to your honorable defense."

"But you don't believe in yourself, do you?" she asked. "Is that why you keep pushing me away?"

Dillon looked down at her trusting face and knew he could never let her go again. "I didn't want to taint you—with my past, with my problems, and I didn't want Eli to do the same."

Frustrated, Isabel refused to back down. "Forget that. I won't let you push me away anymore, not when I can clearly see you need a friend, not a flirtation. I believe you wanted to come home a long time ago. I believe you wanted to be at your father's funeral, but you were too afraid—"

"I'm not afraid."

"Yes, you are. You're so afraid, you'd rather run away than face up to the people you love the most. So you let Eli hurl insults at you and think the worst of you, because that's what you believe about yourself. Am I right?"

He closed his eyes, lifted his face to the wind. "No."

"Yes." She brought her hands back to his face. "Yes."

Dillon could only stand there, staring at her pretty face in the moonlight. The hum of mosquitoes, the sound of distant thunder, the moon's light poking through the scattered clouds above him, everything intensified in her evergreen eyes. And it all reflected the truth she had discovered. Suddenly, he was so tired. So tired of fighting against himself, and against his need to be with her.

"Yes," he said at last, pulling her tightly against him so she couldn't see the shame in his eyes. "Yes, I'm afraid. I did things, Isabel. Horrible things. And now, I've changed, but I don't know how to go about showing everyone I've changed."

Isabel looked him in the eye. "You've already made the first step, Dillon. You came back to Wildwood."

"Yes, I came back—to a brother who hates me, to a mother I've hurt so badly, to a dead father. And to an empty house."

"It's not too late."

He wanted to believe that. He wanted to hold her here forever in his arms and tell her that she'd helped him find a little peace. But, he'd lived on speculation for so long, nothing seemed real anymore. Yet, because she was willing to fight for him, he had found some hope. "Maybe it's *not* too late, after all."

"You've got to believe that," Isabel said. Moving her hands over his face and shoulders, she nodded her head. "Because *I* believe in *you*." She kissed the moisture away from his eyes. "I trust you." She kissed the warm skin on his cheekbone. "I want to help you." She kissed his forehead.

Dillon held back, stiff and unyielding, his eyes drawn tightly shut. He wanted to block her out, wanted to keep this distance between them, even though she could feel the coiled tension rolling inside him like the roaring thunder headed their way.

Her own heart pounding, Isabel drew in a deep

breath. She hadn't wanted to come back here. But then, she'd never expected to find him here, almost as if he'd been waiting for her. Closing her eyes in a silent prayer, she wished she had the strength to walk away. But she'd done that once before. Now, she used her last hope and her faith in God—the faith Grammy had always assured her she did indeed possess, to help this man she cared about so much. "Let me show you, Dillon."

She kissed his lips, closing her eyes to the pain of his indifference. But she felt the quickening of his pulse when her lips met his. Then she lifted her head and said, "We'll find a way, together, with God's help."

Dillon didn't stop to think about the implication of her honesty. Instead, he kissed her, pouring his soul into being able to touch her at last. He wouldn't tell her how he felt, not now. Not yet. He couldn't take that chance. Because he still had some secrets to guard.

Finally, he pulled back, then moved a few feet away, his words lifting out over the night like a soft wind. "You don't know how much that means to me, Issy."

"You can do this," she said, tears choking her words. "That's what faith is all about, Dillon."

He glanced over at her then. "I've been wrestling with my faith and my feelings for you. It just didn't seem possible with all these problems with Eli. I didn't want to drag you into it again."

"I'll be all right," she said, rushing to him, wishing she could hold him close until he learned to trust again. "Let me help you, Dillon."

Dillon lifted her arms away, then walked to the water's edge. Looking down, he asked, "Do you think God has enough love for someone like me? Do you think He's willing to forgive just one more time?"

"I know He is. I believe that with all my heart."

Dillon's chuckle was low and grating. "Then He's sure got his work cut out for Him."

"Grammy always says God can handle anything."

He turned back to her then, reaching out to tug at a wayward blond curl. "And how about you, Isabel? Can you handle anything?"

She swallowed hard, prayed harder. "I can handle you, if that's what you're asking."

"So, you think you can save me, huh?"

The awe in his words fueled her ridiculous hopes. "No, I think you can save yourself."

He lifted his head, then tilted it sideways, eyeing her. "Oh, really. How?"

"You can start by learning to trust again," she suggested. "I'm willing to stay here at Wildwood with you, until you can talk to Eli."

She braced herself, thinking now would be the time to suggest that Eli was in trouble, without actually revealing what she knew. She honestly believed it would be better to let Dillon and his brother work things through without her interference.

"From what Susan tells me, Eli could really use a brother right about now. Maybe if you settle things with him, you can both face your past and get on with your future."

Dillon buried his hands in the pockets of his khakis,

then rocked back on his heels. "You'd do that for me—stay here with me?"

"I will. You and your brother need to get to know each other again. And if that's too hard for you, I'll be here to help you."

"Simply because you care about me?"

"Simply because I told you I wanted to help you."

"We'd be risking everything—Eli won't take too kindly to being waylaid or ambushed. You realize that, don't you?"

"Yes, I realize that. And I think you're wrong. I think Eli needs your help, just as you need mine."

"And yet, you'd still be willing to risk his wrath?"

"Yes." She couldn't tell him that she hoped Dillon and his brother could work this land together. That would be the best solution for everyone right now. But she didn't think Dillon was ready for that step just yet. Maybe with a little nudge, she could ease him into it. Only because tonight, she'd seen how much he needed this land in his life.

And she needed him in her life—she'd realized that tonight, too.

"I can't make you any promises, Isabel," he told her as he pulled her back into his arms.

"You don't have to. I believe in you, remember?"

"It's nice to have someone saying that for a change."

He kissed her, and Isabel savored the gentleness of that kiss. And realized she had fallen back in love with Dillon.

Only this time, it was much more than a schoolgirl crush.

Chapter Eight

"Why don't you come home with me?" Isabel said later as Dillon wheeled the Harley into the dilapidated shed behind the mansion.

It was well past midnight, and while the rain had held off, the sky was now dark with roaming clouds. The night air felt heavy with moisture, humid and waiting—the quiet before the storm.

"On our first date?" he quipped as he helped her off the bike. "Do you think that's wise?"

Isabel smiled at his humor. At least he was in a better mood now. "Silly, that's not what I meant. I want you to talk to my grandmother."

"What?"

"Grammy Martha has a way of making you feel so...good about things," she said, hope in her words. "She'll listen, then she'll hug you so tight, you'll never feel alone again."

He scowled. "Meaning no disrespect to your grandmother, I'd rather be hugging you."

Isabel knew the feeling. But before they could even begin a relationship they needed some guidance and some advice. And her grandmother was an expert on both.

"I'm serious, Dillon," she said, taking his hand to tug him toward the dirt lane. "Grammy can help us through this."

"So, we're just gonna go in and wake your poor old grandmother in the middle of the night, then pour all our troubles at her feet?"

Isabel smiled and bobbed her head. "Something like that, but she won't mind. She's good about things like this. And I, for one, really need to talk to her."

He held back, his words coming low and lifting softly out on the thick air. "About me and how you're willing to stay here and help me? Are you already having doubts about that?"

He still didn't trust her enough to believe her, Isabel realized. He couldn't say the words. He couldn't say "I need you" and he couldn't even say "I trust you." As close as she felt to him right now, Isabel also felt hurt that Dillon could still hold a part of himself back from her. Especially after she'd just realized she was in love with him.

All the more reason to talk to Grammy. She'd bring some perspective to this turmoil. Grammy would know what to do.

"Please, Dillon," Isabel said as they strolled through the sleeping wildflowers. "You need this. You've been out there alone for so long, you don't even know what it's like to have someone to lean on."

"I'm beginning to see what it can be like, though,"

he said, his fingers squeezing hers tightly. "And I'm starting to appreciate it."

"Then come inside with me. We'll raid the cookie jar and talk to Grammy."

"You lead an exciting life, Isabel."

She saw his grin and laughed. "Yeah, always on the edge. That's me."

He tugged her around as they reached the back door, his expression changing from cynical to serious. "We were both on the edge, weren't we? Until we came back here and found each other again."

"I think you're right," Isabel said, loving him all the more for being just a little honest at least. "I don't know...lately I've been so restless. My work is still important and fulfilling, but I seem to be drifting...not quite sure which way I need to go next." She shrugged, then looked out over the distant cotton fields. "I think that's why I agreed to come here and be a part of this wedding. I didn't realize it, but I needed to see Wildwood again, just to make peace with myself. And as much as I always wanted to get away from here, I have to admit it feels good to know I have a place to call home."

Dillon looked out into the night, out toward the looming shadow of the house he'd lived in as a child. "But I don't."

"Yes, you do," she said, careful that he didn't bolt on her. "You can rebuild Wildwood, Dillon. Have you ever thought about that?"

"Every waking minute of my life," he said on a rush of breath. "I've been thinking of doing a little touch-up work while I'm here. But—"

"You won't fail," she replied, guessing his doubts. "I know you won't."

"What makes you so sure? You don't know where I've been all these years, the things I've done—"

"I know everything I need to know. And I don't believe you've done anything terrible. Sure, you've made mistakes, but you've obviously accomplished a lot. You're a self-made man, Dillon. Whatever brought you to this point, I believe you're a better man for it."

"You amaze me," he said, tugging her close for a quick kiss. "And I do believe I'd like to wake up your grandmother and have some milk and cookies, just so I can tell her what her granddaughter has done for me."

"What have I done?" she had to ask.

"You've made me face my greatest hopes and my worst fears. Not bad for a night's work."

Isabel turned to open the door, afraid he'd see the truth in her eyes. What would he do if he knew she was deliberately setting him up to help his brother? What would he do if he found out that Eli was close to losing everything Dillon had ever held dear? She should just tell him, but then he'd lash out at Eli and they'd be right back where they'd started. No, better to let him ease into things. Better to let him make the decisions, call the shots. Yet she couldn't help but feel small and deceitful.

I'm doing it for him, Lord, she said silently. *He needs his home again.* Selfishly, she reminded herself that she needed Dillon. Was that why she was willing to pull him—and herself—back into Wildwood's uncertain arms? Just so she could keep him near?

No, it was more than that. Dillon wanted to be back here at his home. And she was determined to make his dream come true. Only, she had to wonder if the end justified the means.

They didn't have to wake Martha Landry. She was sitting in the small den, reading her Bible.

"Hi, Grammy," Isabel said as she poked her head around the door frame. "Feel like some company?"

Not missing a beat, Martha finished the verse she'd been studying, then placed her hand-crocheted book-mark across the page to keep her place. "Of course. Who'd you bring home?"

Isabel yanked a reluctant Dillon into the room, beaming with pride. "It's Dillon, Grammy."

"Well, well." Getting up out of her padded re-cliner, Martha automatically opened her arms. "Dil-lon Murdock, come here and give me a hug. It's so good to see you again."

Shocked and clearly uncomfortable, Dillon strolled across the rickety wooden floor to place tentative hands around Martha's rounded shoulders. "Hello, Mrs. Landry."

Martha gave him a good hug, her eyes smiling over at her granddaughter while she held Dillon's hand tightly in hers. "And what have you two been up to this late at night?"

Dillon stood back, unsure how to begin. He had a lump in his throat the size of a watermelon just from hugging the woman. If he actually unburdened him-self on her, he'd probably cry like a baby and make a complete idiot of himself. Glancing over at Isabel for help, he could only stand there and wonder what had come over him. He didn't understand why being hugged should have such an effect on him but he wasn't so sure he wanted to open himself up to it completely. So he just stood there, his head down, his lips pressed together, his eyes centered on Isabel.

"Uh, we went to the rehearsal dinner, of course," Isabel began, motioning for Dillon to take a seat next to her on the couch.

"How did that go?" Martha asked, her expression pricelessly bland, her hands folded primly in front of her.

"Not too good," Dillon blurted out. Then, frustrated with himself, he sliced fingers through the spikes of his dark hair. "I...I made a scene."

"Did you now?"

"Yes, ma'am. I guess I really messed things up—again."

"Eli messed things up," Isabel retorted. "He could have been more civil and forgiving."

"Well," Martha said, her eyes widening, "we can't mess up things so bad that The Lord can't help fix them. How 'bout I get us some lemonade—it's too humid and hot for coffee, isn't it?" Already padding toward the kitchen, she called, "And Isabel, you can bring out those ladyfingers we had left from the shower."

"Okay," Isabel said, glancing over at Dillon to make sure he wasn't about to head out the door. Sitting there on her grandmother's couch, his stormy eyes wide and searching, he looked so much like the young boy she remembered. "Are you all right?"

"I think so," he said, gratitude in the words. "I'll come help with the cookies."

She smiled at him, then reached over to pat his hand. "It's going to be okay, Dillon."

"Is it, really?"

"Yes."

"Tomorrow night's my brother's wedding."

"Yes, and you'll be the best usher there."

"If I show up. It seems pretty clear that Eli doesn't want me there," he said, following Isabel into the kitchen.

"Dillon, come and eat some cookies," she told him.

"You're not going to let me get out of this, are you?"

"No," Isabel said after settling him at the small dining table. "If I have to be there, so do you."

"Hey, Mrs. Landry," he said, his smile wry, "did you know your granddaughter has decided to be my champion, my defender, my lady of the realm?"

Martha poured him a tall glass of fresh squeezed lemonade. Looking down at him with wise eyes and her own wry smile, she nodded. "Hey, Dillon, did you know that my granddaughter has always been on your side?"

He looked across the table at Isabel, his heart skipping a beat at her beauty. "No, I didn't know that. But I sure wish I had."

And he had to wonder—could Isabel possibly feel something beyond friendship for him? Could she possibly love him in the same way he loved her? Was that why she was so willing to fight for him, to help him mend his torn family? And did she know that he had always loved her? How could he tell her that he'd fallen for her way back in their high school days, or maybe even beyond. If he told her that, then he'd have to tell her the ugly truth about his leaving Wildwood.

Martha patted his hand, surprising him so much he almost spilled his lemonade. Then she settled down in her favorite chair and reached for a crescent shaped, sugar-dusted cookie. "Now, children, tell me why you're keeping an old lady up so late."

Isabel told her grandmother what had happened at the rehearsal dinner. "Eli was downright rude, Grammy. I felt really bad for Miss Cynthia."

"She is trying to bring her family back together," Martha said, dusting the powdered sugar off her fingers. Turning to gaze at Dillon, she asked, "How do you feel about all of this?"

With a shrug, he said, "I think I should have stayed in Atlanta."

Martha nodded. "You think that would make things easier for everyone?"

"I do believe so, yes."

"And what about your mother? You know, she's talked about this wedding—and you being a part of it—for months now."

Dillon lifted his head then, his eyes slamming both Martha and Isabel with pain and denial. "They don't want me here, not really."

Martha leaned forward a bit, adjusting herself on her chair. "Your mother certainly does. And, your brother could use your help right now."

Surprised, Dillon snorted. "That's exactly what Isabel has been telling me. But I don't believe it. Eli has always been able to land on his feet. I used to think he really needed me, but I finally figured out he's never needed anyone's help, especially mine. And after all this time, I'm the last person he'd want around.''

"Now how do you know that?"

Dillon looked around the worn old kitchen. This was where Isabel had spent her childhood. Right here, on Wildwood, just like him. Yet he only had to glance around at the faded curtains and the cracked kitchen sink to know that they'd lived completely different lives. The guilt of that realization ate away at him, causing him to remember things he'd tried so hard to forget.

Instead of answering Martha's question, he looked over at Isabel. "You had it all, Issy. Did you know that?''

Isabel's head shot up. "What do you mean?"

Dillon lifted his hands, then let them fall across the table. "Look at us, sitting here in the kitchen in the middle of the night. This could never have happened in my house, in my family. No, there everything was so formal, so stilted, everything in its place—Murdock's don't show great displays of emotion. Murdocks *don't* sit around the kitchen, munching on cookies.''

"Are you uncomfortable?" she asked defensively, wondering if he found it distasteful to be here in this shack of a house.

"Yes. No. What I'm trying to tell you is that while I grew up in the mansion, you had the real home. Do you know how lucky you are?''

Isabel felt as if she'd just been pinned to the wall. "I've never thought about it. I've certainly never considered myself lucky.''

"No, because all you could think about was how poor you were, how you wanted to get away from here, to have a better life? Is your life better now, Isabel?"

Confused by his questions, and more than a little angry that he was giving her the third degree, she asked, "Why are you turning the tables, Dillon? Grammy asked *you* a question."

"And I'm trying to answer her."

"By telling me how lucky I am?"

"Yes!" He shoved a hand through his hair, then sat back to look at her. "Do you know how many times I wished my father would just hug me, or tell me he was proud of me? Oh, he bragged to his friends, of course. But he never really showed either of us much real affection. Not like this, not the way your grandmother shows you affection."

Bitterness coloring his words, he said, "And he passed his misguided traits on to Eli, too. Do you know what it's like when your only brother won't even speak to you, that if you try to call just to hear a voice from home, he'll only hang up on you?"

Isabel saw the torment in his eyes, but couldn't believe a brother could treat another brother that way. "Eli did that?"

"The few times I called and he answered, yes."

Bringing a hand to her mouth, Isabel sank back on her chair. "I never knew it was *that* bad between you two."

"Well, it was, and it still is," he said on a low, calm breath. "Your parents loved you, Isabel. Sure, they were old-fashioned and strict, but they loved you. And they showed you that every day. Me, I had to search for any traces of real love in my dad's eyes. His love always came with certain conditions. I don't think he was ever really proud of me—he just tolerated me because of my mother, and he presented a solid front for everyone else, for the Murdock name. We couldn't have anyone thinking things weren't perfect in the Murdock household.'' Dropping his shoulders, he added, ''So, I guess you both know how I feel about things now, huh?''

Martha sat silent, her gaze moving from her granddaughter's surprised face to Dillon's resigned one.

Isabel shook her head, her eyes widening as she tried to reason with Dillon. ''But he had to have loved you. Why, he gave you and Eli everything, without question.''

''No, he *bought* us things, Issy. There's a big difference. It was almost like he was paying us off, for being what he expected us to be. And when I failed, well—''

Martha said the same thing Isabel had said earlier. ''Everyone thought you were his favorite, the way he defended you.''

''In public, yeah. He had an image to maintain. He and mother always put such high store in appearances. But I made one slip too many, though, and suddenly, I was no longer the image of a perfect son. I guess he realized all the glossing over in the world couldn't change how I felt the day we had that terrible argument. And I fell out of his favor pretty quick after that.''

''One slip too many?'' Shaking her head again, Isabel got up to pace the room. ''Dillon, you made some mistakes, but your father always forgave you.

Maybe if you'd stayed here, it would have all worked out.''

"I don't think so. Not this time. I used to get into trouble, yeah," Dillon said, nodding. "But that was different. That didn't involve turning against my family. My father demanded loyalty, and...in the end, I couldn't give it to him."

Placing her hands on the table, Isabel asked, "What did he want you to do? What on earth happened?"

Dillon looked up then, his expression going blank. Raising up with a push, he headed for the door. "I've got to go. I've said too much as it is."

"Dillon?"

He turned at the door, pushing her away. "I appreciate the talk, ladies. Let's just get through this wedding. I'll see you both tomorrow." Before Isabel could speak, he nodded to Martha. "Thanks for the refreshments, and thanks for listening."

With that, he was gone, gently closing the screen door behind him. Isabel watched as he made his way down the wildflower path, back toward the old mansion.

"What's the matter with him?" she said, throwing her hands up in the air. "Why can't he tell me what's bothering him?"

Martha came to stand by her granddaughter. "I think I understand what's wrong with Dillon."

"Then please explain it to me. I thought we'd made some progress."

"Isabel, he doesn't want to reveal the Murdock family secrets. Whatever happened that day, Dillon is still trying to honor his father by keeping quiet about it. He has to make his own peace with his brother, and especially, with himself.''

Whirling around, Isabel said, ''Am I just supposed to sit back and wait for that to happen? I've got a bad feeling about all of this—this wedding, Eli's attitude, Dillon's indifference. I'm telling you, something has got to give.''

''Since when do you care so much about the Murdocks, anyway?'' Martha asked as she put away the cookie tin.

Isabel turned to face her all-knowing grandmother then. Too late to deny what was so obvious now. ''I've always cared about Dillon. And since we've been back together, well...''

''You love him, don't you?''

Wrapping her arms across her chest, Isabel lowered her head and nodded. ''I don't want to—but, yes, I guess I do. I think I've always loved him.''

''So you'll fight for him?''

''If he'll let me.''

''And who will you be fighting?''

''I don't know. Eli, mostly, I guess. I want Dillon to be happy again, but Eli disapproves of me so much. If I get involved, it's only going to make matters worse.''

''You might be getting into something you can't fix, child. We have to choose our battles very carefully.''

Isabel rushed to her grandmother's side then. ''Help me, Grammy. Tell me how to make those two stubborn men see that it's time to end this grudge.''

Martha patted Isabel's shoulder, then stood back.

"Does Dillon know Eli's been having some troubles?"

Shocked, Isabel let out a breath. "No, and how do you know that?"

"I hear things. This is a small town, Isabel. Rumors are grist for the mill around here."

Glad to be able to share this burden, Isabel nodded. "Susan told me about it. She thinks Dillon should stay here and help Eli out. I wanted to talk to Dillon about it, but he'll be so upset and bitter. I don't know what to do."

Martha hugged her close. "For now, go to bed and pray. The Lord will help you—even if it means you just have to stay out of it."

"I have to help Dillon."

"I don't think Dillon is ready for your help."

"Then I'll wait."

"You never were good at waiting."

Hugging her grandmother close, Isabel said, "Dillon was right about one thing. I never realized how blessed I was, living here. Why couldn't I see that, Grammy?"

"You had too many dreams, honey. Too many stars in your eyes."

Isabel watched as Martha headed down the tiny hallway toward the back of the creaking house. Then she turned to stare over at Wildwood, her heart breaking. Yes, she'd certainly had stars in her eyes. Maybe because she didn't even realize until she was around six years old that her father didn't own the land he worked. She didn't realize until she got to school and saw all the other children laughing and playing, that she was just a poor country bumpkin who got teased because of her homemade dresses and hand-me-down cast-off clothes. Soon, she'd discovered the world beyond Wildwood, and she'd promised herself she'd explore that world and conquer it. But was she any richer for having done so?

She should just pack up and leave right now. She'd told herself not to get involved, yet here she stood, worried and confused, and right in the thick of things between Dillon and Eli. But, she couldn't leave.

Because she was in love with Dillon Murdock.

"I'll wait," she whispered to the whining wind. "I'll wait right here, Lord, until You show me what to do."

Just then, a light flickered to life in an upstairs window of the mansion. Isabel watched as the shadowy silhouette of a man appeared at the window.

Dillon.

She watched as he stood there, his hands braced on the windowsill, looking out into the night. Was he looking for her? Was he thinking about her?

Dillon had come so close to telling her everything. But something kept holding him back, something kept him from being honest with her and maybe with himself. What kind of pain had Eli and their father inflicted on him? Why had he felt it so necessary to run away from his home? Somehow, she had to find a way to get inside his head, to understand why he was afraid to love her the way she loved him.

Until then, she'd have to be patient. She'd wait.

She watched his shadow, so still, so clear, so dark there against that single lamplight.

And then she knew. He was waiting, too.

Chapter Nine

Dillon was up at dawn the next day. Actually, he'd never really fallen asleep. Instead, he'd lain in bed listening as the thunder moved farther to the south. The rain had missed Wildwood, and Dillon now missed the rain.

He needed a good cloudburst to relieve some of the tension that had kept him awake all night. Today was his brother's wedding day, but that was the least of his worries.

He loved her.

And now, he wanted her to love him, too.

Isabel Landry had told him she wanted to stand by him, but could she ever return the love he felt for her?

Now he had to decide what he was going to do about this love he'd so long denied. His initial reaction had been pure joy. But, it was a joy born of long ago dreams and long forgotten hopes. Since leaving Wildwood, he'd tried to put Isabel out of his mind—

for her sake. She deserved better than him; she deserved so much more than he could ever give her.

Taking another sip of coffee, Dillon sat back on the ratty cane rocker he'd found in the attic and pulled onto the porch, wondering if he'd ever be capable of accepting love from any woman. Oh, he loved Isabel, knew that in his heart. But in his head, logic told him he shouldn't acknowledge that love. He couldn't ask her to take him on; he couldn't ask her to accept his family into her heart.

So here he sat, wishing, wondering if he should just leave soon after the wedding, or stay and pour his heart and soul into rebuilding this old house, and winning over the woman of his dreams. Could he actually have both?

Right now, that didn't seem possible. She'd promised to stand by him, to help him reconcile with his brother. But what Isabel didn't know was that she couldn't help him. She'd only make matters worse.

But Dillon couldn't tell her that. He couldn't tell Isabel that *she* was one of the main reasons he and his brother were no longer on speaking terms.

Throwing the dregs of his coffee out into the overgrown shrubbery, Dillon stood to go inside. That's when he saw Eli and two other men standing in Eli's front yard. All three were looking a little too keenly toward the old mansion. Stepping back out of view, Dillon watched as Eli talked in an animated fashion, his hands gesturing, his face flushed with anger.

"What are you up to, brother?" Dillon muttered. The men sure seemed interested in the old plantation house. Squinting toward the fresh rising eastern sun, Dillon recognized one of the men. Leland Burke. The president of Wildwood Bank and Trust, complete with suit, tie and a notebook. Dillon watched as Leland jotted down information. He didn't recognize the other man.

Now, what was so important that Eli would be standing out here on a Saturday morning, on his wedding day, at that?

Isabel glanced out the window over the kitchen sink, wondering what Eli was doing standing out in his front yard. From her vantage point, the three men were nearly obstructed by trees and bushes, and she had to crane her neck to even see them at all. But there was no doubt in her mind that one of them was Eli Murdock.

Shrugging, she guessed Eli had to conduct business, even on his wedding day. Running a huge plantation was a twenty-four hour job. She could remember lots of times when her father would stay out in the fields well past dark, then come home and collapse before rising with the dawn to get a head start on the next day's work. That grueling schedule had put him in an early grave. A few years later, it had also taken Eli and Dillon's father, Roy, to his grave.

She had to agree with Susan. If Eli didn't slow down, he might wind up the same way. He did look rather haggard. Of course, he had aged since Isabel had been away. They were all getter older. But after what Susan had told her, she supposed Eli's pallor had more to do with worry than age.

All the more reason to bring peace to the Murdock brothers, she mused as she finished washing the breakfast dishes. Looking out toward the rising sun, she sent up a prayer for help.

"Should I tell Dillon what I know about Eli's financial problems? Or should I do as Grammy says and keep praying about it?"

If she told Dillon, he might confront Eli, and Eli would only resent her even more for interfering. Yet, Dillon had a right to know that his home was in jeopardy.

Isabel didn't know how to approach this. Dillon was still struggling with his past, and after last night, she knew in her heart that underneath his tough guy veneer, there was a heart that longed to come home. Dillon needed to be accepted back into his family completely.

If he found out about Eli's financial woes, that acceptance would be shattered. Yet he was bound to hear about it sooner or later.

"After the wedding," she said on a breathless whisper. "Once Eli's away on his honeymoon, maybe I can talk to Dillon about this."

That would give him time to cool down before he confronted his brother. In the meantime, Isabel had a job to do. She had to be at the church early to capture the entire wedding party in various shots. Susan would be frantic if Isabel didn't arrive on time to photograph every aspect of this important day.

So much fuss over a mere wedding. Isabel had never given her own wedding day much thought, maybe because she'd never pictured herself as a beaming bride. Thinking of Dillon and how his kisses made her feel, she closed her eyes and had a fine little daydream of her own.

She was standing in the wildflowers in a creamy gown and Dillon was walking toward her with that sideways slant in his eyes, and that precious grin on his handsome face. He carried a bouquet of wildflowers—pinks and blues, yellows and whites—picked especially for her. Birds were singing, bees were buzzing and the sunset behind them was so brilliant it hurt her eyes. So brilliant—

"Too brilliant," she said now, snapping back to reality. "Just a silly dream, Issy. It can never happen, no matter how hard you wish it."

Chastising herself, she remembered her duties. This was Susan's big day, not hers. She wouldn't let her friend down.

But she hoped she didn't let Dillon down either.

Hours later, Isabel looked about at everyone who'd assembled at the church for the big event. And big it was. Looking around the sun-dappled sanctuary, she was amazed at the expense that had obviously been put into this wedding. The Murdocks never did anything second-rate, and while the Websters were comfortable financially, Isabel imagined they broke the bank trying to accommodate Eli and Cynthia Murdock's demands.

The theme was Victorian, about as delicate and dainty as a theme could get, complete with hearts, pearls, flowers and lace. Pinkish-white day lilies with rich burgundy centers, and pink roses in tight cotton-candy clusters, adorned the pews and the altar, while baby's breath and white satin ribbons scattered throughout complimented the fragrant flowers. Candles burned from exquisite silver candelabra, complimenting the bridesmaids' muted pink lace-trimmed dresses. Isabel had to admit the barely-there pink was pretty and a little more subtle than the bright teal Susan had originally picked. But she'd give Miss Cynthia more credit for that, than Eli's bullying Susan to change things.

Standing back in a corner, Isabel mentally went over her last-minute list. She'd taken the obligatory shots of the bride and her bridesmaids, and the groom and his best man. Eli had actually smiled into the camera, but his smile didn't hide the bright worry Isabel now recognized in his unforgiving eyes. She supposed it was her good fortune that Eli was so pre-occupied with his wedding and his debts that he didn't have the inclination to pick on her.

She could almost feel sorry for Eli. He seemed to really care about Susan, and Isabel believed he wanted to make his new bride happy by putting up a good front at this wedding. But the pressure had to be tremendous. She wondered how long he could keep all these balls in the air. So far, he'd done a passable job, other than refusing to welcome Dillon back home as his mother had requested. Obviously, Eli didn't want Dillon to find out about his troubles. He had way too much pride to ask for his brother's help.

At least Dillon was still part of the wedding party.

Because this was a Murdock wedding, and because the whole town was talking about the famous grudge between the two brothers, the turnout for today's nup-tials had reached maximum capacity. It seemed as if everyone in town who'd been invited had made it a priority to attend. Dillon, along with the other ushers, had escorted a steady stream of well-heeled, curious guests to their seats.

Isabel watched now as he held the arm of an elderly woman wearing a bright floral ensemble complete with a yellow pillbox hat. His hand was steady on the woman's plump arm, his demeanor respectful and charming as he talked with the lady in quiet, animated tones. Isabel snapped a picture as Dillon walked by. She wanted to capture that not-so-innocent grin.

Putting her camera down, she took a deep breath. They hadn't spoken since last night. Things had been too hectic for more than a polite nod. But behind the nod and the quiet looks, she could see the darkness in Dillon's eyes. In spite of their new closeness, she believed he was still holding something back.

Wishing she could gain his complete trust, Isabel continued to watch him. He looked so handsome in his tuxedo—a paradox of a man, gentle and shy in some ways, bold and unyielding in others. To the manor born, but so down-to-earth and unassuming about his own success.

In many ways, Dillon had changed. In many ways, he was still the same. And she would always love him. Now that she'd accepted that, she felt a little more at peace. Underneath the turmoil, underneath the fear and worry, her center was settling into a nice contentment. She'd denied her feelings for Dillon for so long now, that she realized she'd been empty inside. But since coming back here, since seeing him again and accepting that she cared about him, that emptiness was gradually easing away. Grammy had always told her she'd find peace once she focused on what really mattered in life. And Dillon was what mattered in hers.

Soon, they'd both be leaving Wildwood. But somehow, after last night, Isabel didn't feel as strongly about leaving the place she'd once called home.

Wanting to understand why Dillon was still keeping her at arm's length, she continued to study him now. And again wondered if maybe Dillon didn't care about her in the same way she cared for him. Maybe he was trying to let her down gently. Maybe his flirtation *was* just that, a flirtation, a way to spend time while he was forced to be here. She'd certainly seen him tease many a young girl way back when, only to leave another broken heart in his wake. What if that part of him hadn't changed after all?

But, no, that couldn't be right. Last night, he'd opened up to her a little bit, at least. Dillon cared about her, he'd admitted that much. Yet, she knew in her soul he was fighting his feelings. Why?

Moaning, Isabel took a step back as the crowd continued to grow. Lifting her camera, she automatically clicked several shots of the various guests, making sure she got the most prominent ones, as Susan had suggested. The whole while, Isabel kept thinking what if she'd been wrong, hoping Dillon might actually feel something real for her. Sure, he'd kissed her with a tenderness that made her heart palpitate, but that was part of Dillon's charm. At times, he'd sought her out; other times, he'd sent her away. Had it all been a game, like the silly games they used to play when they were growing up?

She looked up then, to find Dillon's gray eyes centered on her with all the gentleness of a dove. As he came toward her, her heart picked up its tempo. The expression on his face told her he did care, and the look in his eyes changed from gentle to tumultuous within the fraction of a lazy blink.

"Hello, gorgeous," he said, his gaze moving across her face with unabashed intensity. "Why are you hiding in the corner?"

"Just doing my job," she quipped, the catch in her voice causing her to groan silently.

"Listen, about last night—"

"I thought we'd reached some sort of truce last night," she replied as she checked her camera. "Was I wrong?"

"No. You really got to me last night, Issy. I'm through running, but hey, I'm still a little skittish. Just give me some time. I promise, after this shindig is over, we're going to have a long talk."

Her heart soared with new hope. "I'll hold you to that." And maybe then, she could tell him about his brother's troubles.

He nodded, then his features relaxed into a grin. "You should be center stage; you look much prettier than the bride."

"How do you know—you haven't peeked into the bride's dressing room, now have you?"

"I don't have to see her. Susan's the cute cheerleader type, but she doesn't hold a candle to you. A bit too frilly for me, I'm afraid. I like *your* dress, Issy."

"You said that same thing at the rehearsal dinner, if I recall, and I also recall—you dated a lot of frilly cheerleaders in high school."

"You looked good at the rehearsal dinner, too, if I

recall, and yes, I went out with a few cheerleaders, but hey, none of them could handle having a cad like me for their steady.'' Lifting a dark brow, he said, ''Maybe because they all figured out I really preferred a tall, willowy artistic blonde with wild curls and not a spot of lace anywhere on her dress. I like all of your dresses, but this one is especially nice—green becomes you.''

Looking down at the flowing skirt of her tea-length crepe gown, Isabel pushed at the unruly curls he'd just complimented and shrugged. ''This old thing— plain and simple and very functional for a working girl.''

''That old thing brings out the green in your eyes, and you know it.'' Coming closer, he said in a low, gravelly tone, ''I'm sorry I left in such a huff last night.''

''Stop apologizing. I understand.''

His brow furrowed. ''Are you okay?''

She shook her head. ''I'm fine. I want to get through this, so we can talk.''

''I know the feeling. Remember, you promised me a dance at the reception.''

Her heart started the dance without her. ''I remember.''

''Okay. I've got to get back to ushering, or I might get fired.''

''See you later.''

He gave her his salute. ''Count on it.''

She would. And she hoped she could count on him. She'd wait for him, but she wouldn't force him into a relationship he might not be ready to accept. There were too many things brewing in the air, too much standing in the way of any happiness for Dillon and her. Her love for him had made her temporarily forget all the obstacles holding them apart, the same obstacles that had been there from the very beginning. Namely, his brother's intense disapproval of her.

Loving Dillon hadn't changed a thing, except she now realized she'd been waiting for him most of her life.

And, as her grandmother had pointed out, Isabel wasn't very good at waiting.

The wedding was lovely. Susan made a pretty bride in her beaded frock and elaborate veil. Eli was a handsome groom in spite of the occasional scowl he shot toward his brother. He did seem nervous and preoccupied to Isabel, though. As he promised to love, honor and cherish his bride, Isabel said a prayer for him—a first for her. She'd never considered including Eli Murdock in her prayers. But Susan had always been a good friend to her, in spite of their different positions in small-town society, and the romantic in Isabel wanted this marriage to work. She'd be wrong to hope for that without asking God to watch over both Susan and Eli. And Dillon, too.

Careful not to be intrusive, Isabel took a picture of the groom kissing his new bride. Automatically, she searched for Dillon and found him watching her with that unreadable, brooding look on his face. But when he lifted his gaze to her face, Isabel saw the darkness disappear. His eyes became bright with hope and longing.

Feeling silly over her earlier misgivings, she again reassured herself that he did care. But, something wasn't quite right. It was as if Dillon wanted to return her feelings, but he couldn't give himself permission to do so just yet.

He said we'd talk after the wedding, she reminded herself as she watched Eli and Susan walk back down the aisle. This whole event had been a strain on everyone, as blessed as it was, but now it was just about finished.

She'd use the few days Susan and Eli were away to organize her pictures. She wanted to have a complete set of contact sheets ready for Susan when she got home. And, she'd be able to spend time with Dillon, alone, without Eli's condemning eyes watching over them. Maybe then, she could find out what exactly was on his mind, and what exactly was in his heart.

And after that...she'd do whatever she could to help Dillon mend his torn relationship with his brother.

Because if Dillon and Eli could mend their fences, there might be hope for Isabel and Dillon, at last. Maybe that was what was holding Dillon back from giving her his love.

"Did you get a lot of pictures of us at the altar?" Susan asked much later at the reception.

The church social hall was decorated in the same Victorian theme as the sanctuary had been, with muted pinks and blues and roses, hearts, seed pearls and baby's breath scattered among ribbons and lace. The wedding cake carried the theme to new heights, all five tiered layers of it.

"I promise, you'll have the biggest, best wedding

album of any woman in the state of Georgia," Isabel assured the fidgeting bride. "Now, relax. The wedding was so beautiful and you were the perfect bride."

Susan swiped at fresh tears. "I'm being so silly. I can't stop crying. Hope you didn't get any pictures of my puffy eyes."

"I got you in your very best light," Isabel again assured her. "I should have most of them developed by the time you get back from Saint Simons Island."

Susan frowned, then lowered her voice. "I'm just glad I was able to pull Eli away from this place for a few days. Have you talked to Dillon yet?"

Glancing around, Isabel saw Dillon talking to his mother. Eli was deep in a discussion with two other local farmers. "I've tried, Susan, but I'm afraid if I'm the one to bring it all up, Eli and Dillon both will resent me for interfering. I really would rather not get involved."

Susan touched Isabel's arm, her hand cold in spite of the warm day outside. "You've got to let him know, Isabel. Eli needs his brother's help."

"But do you realize how angry Eli might be? Having Dillon learn the plantation's in trouble can only make matters worse between him and Dillon."

"Tell him while we're away. He can watch over things while we're gone, and maybe by the time we get back, he'll be calmed down enough to talk to Eli and offer his help."

"You're sure optimistic."

"Just hopeful. I want those two to reconcile, too."

Before Isabel could reply, she turned to see Dillon coming across the room. He extended his hand to her as the ensemble of musicians began to play a beautiful classical waltz.

"It's Mozart," Dillon said into her ear, his eyes warm. "And I asked them to play it just for us." When Isabel hesitated, he added, "Hey, I asked you for a dance the night of my senior prom, remember? And you turned me down. You aren't going to do that to me again, are you, Issy?"

Isabel swallowed the lump in her throat. "No. I'll be happy to dance with you, Dillon."

He took her into his arms and whirled her around the dance floor. Isabel gazed up into his eyes, aware that the entire room, full of prominent Wildwood citizens, was watching them as they moved to the exquisite music. Her dress flared out behind her like green sea foam. Her hair lifted away from her damp neck. Her hand touched on the corded muscles of Dillon's arm, while her other hand held tightly to his. The dance became a breathless kind of wonder, a fantasy come true, a sweet memory that she'd lived and relived, and had now become a reality. She was dancing with Dillon Murdock.

"Why did you turn me down that night?" he asked now, his words lifting out over the strands of the music, his eyes centered on her with that brilliant intensity that took her breath away. "Why, Isabel?"

Isabel looked down at the neat black bow tie at his neck, afraid he'd see the truth there in her eyes.

"Tell me the truth," he said.

She met his eyes then, her face inches from his. How could she answer such a question. Should she just blurt it out? Because I was in love with you. No. Not yet. Hating the catch that clutched at her words, she said in what she hoped was a light tone, "I couldn't bear it, Dillon. I couldn't dance with *you*— the boy who'd chased me around with spiders and lizards, the boy who'd beat me too many times at baseball in the back pasture."

The music stopped then, but Dillon didn't let her go. Instead, he pulled her close, his hands moving over her hair as he stood there with her in the center of the hushed room. Isabel held her breath, thinking he was going to do something really stupid like kiss her. But he didn't. Instead, he just held her, his eyes, bright with regret, bright with need, searching her face.

"No more games," he said as he lifted a finger to touch a curl falling away from her temple. "We're adults now, remember? And I do believe the rules have changed. This is a little more challenging than backyard baseball, isn't it?"

She nodded. "We've changed, but some things are still the same. I guess, I've always felt that I don't deserve you, Dillon. Maybe that's the real reason I didn't dance with you at the prom."

She watched as he let that admission soak in.

Then he shook his head. "You've got that all backwards, Issy. *I* don't deserve you. Thanks for the dance, though. I've always wondered what it would be like to dance with you in my arms—it was wonderful."

With that, he turned and stalked across the room and out the door, leaving Isabel in the middle of the empty dance floor, with the roar of whispers in her ears as everyone there talked and pointed and smirked.

She looked up to find Eli watching her, the smug expression on his face like a hard slap across her flushed skin. Moving in on her, he said, "You just can't seem to understand, Isabel. Dillon will never settle down with one woman. Nothing will ever come of his pretty words, no matter how hard you try to cling to him. He'll be gone before sunrise, honey. Just like before. I can promise you that." His eyes flickered over her with a look close to disgust. "At least then, we'll all be rid of both of you and these embarrassing public displays."

Humiliated, Isabel managed to make her way to the ladies' room, her head held high. She didn't know what was going on here, but tomorrow morning, she intended to have it out with Dillon Murdock one way or another. And she'd tell him all about his brother in the process. Maybe if he knew the truth, he'd finally tell her what his problem was.

He didn't think he deserved her; well, she certainly didn't deserve to be held one moment, then pushed away the next. Each time she thought she and Dillon had grown closer, he retreated behind that distant, stony wall again.

She had to find out why. In the meantime, she'd go home and talk to Grammy. She needed someone to help her with her prayers. She needed all the prayers she and her grandmother could muster. And then some.

They all did.

Chapter Ten

Isabel went to church with her grandmother Sunday morning, then came home determined to find Dillon and get the air cleared between them. Even the preacher's sermon had seemed delivered just for her.

"Let all that you do be done with love."

That had been the Bible verse for the sermon, straight out of the first chapter of Corinthians. The preacher had talked about courage, strength, overcoming fear and obstacles. Well, she intended to overcome her fears and all the obstacles holding Dillon and her apart. Beginning with his thorny relationship with his brother. Dillon had to know the truth, and it looked as if she would have to be the one to tell him. It was wrong for Dillon to go on punishing himself for past deeds, when Eli was just as guilty of mismanaging the Murdock fortune as his brother seemed to think he'd been.

"Still worried?" Martha asked as they finished putting away the brunch dishes.

"Yes," Isabel had to admit. "And I really appreciate your listening to me whine last night, Grammy."

"That's part of a grandmother's job," Martha replied. Untying her apron, she yawned. "But all these late nights you young people keep have caught up with me. I'm going to take a long Sunday afternoon nap."

Isabel gave her grandmother a hug. "Good idea. And I'm going to go and find Dillon. Do you think I'm doing the right thing?"

Martha hung her apron on a nearby peg. "I'm beginning to think he needs to know—maybe he can help his brother out of this mess. Eli has just about reached the end of the road. Everything crumbles if the foundation isn't solid. Remember the parable, Isabel, the one about the sower and how some of the seeds fell on the wayside, but some fell on good ground?"

Isabel nodded.

"Well, Wildwood is good ground, honey. The best. And this land has belonged to the Murdocks for well over a century now. Eli means well, but his heart has hardened. He's lost his way."

"But how can we help him, if he doesn't want our help?" Isabel asked. "Eli is so stubborn, and he's a snob to boot!"

"Yes, but we have to be steadfast. We have to remember that we have always lived on this land, too."

"Eli doesn't care about us, Grammy. Why, he'd just as soon we were off this land for good, as let us help him."

"We can't stand by any longer, though," Martha

said, worry creasing her usually serene face. "In spite of our good intentions to stay out of Murdock business, we can't forget that Cynthia will certainly need us."

Isabel had to agree there. "Poor Miss Cynthia doesn't have a clue as to what's really going on. She's been rich and pampered for so long, she won't know how to handle things if they lose this place."

"Give her some credit, Isabel. Cynthia Murdock is made of strong stock. This will shock her, of course, and she'll be deeply humiliated and embarrassed, but if we offer her our support, she'll come through just fine. She'll survive and be a better woman for it."

"If you think so."

"You have to have faith, honey. Faith that this will work out for the best," Martha said.

"But...if they lose everything...Dillon will be devastated. I don't know if he and Eli will ever overcome their differences if that happens."

"Well, people go through these types of crises every day. Many a Georgia farmer has had to lay awake at night wondering how he was going to feed his family."

"Daddy sure did his share of worrying, didn't he?"

"He did, since his pay depended on how good the Murdock crop turned out each year. But he always took the high road. Remember that, Isabel."

"Yes, ma'am. I will."

Isabel watched as her grandmother shuffled off down the hall, wondering why Grammy always made such pointed remarks. There was so much she didn't understand about her gentle, caring parents. She needed answers, not just from Dillon, but from her grandmother, too.

Maybe then, she could find the same sense of peace Grammy seemed to possess. Maybe then, she could make her own peace with Wildwood, at last.

She found Dillon in the middle of the great old house, sitting on the floor against a wall, the portable stereo playing some jazzy instrumental tune. His head was back, his eyes closed while he swayed to the music.

Watching him from the open back door, in spite of her confusion and anger, Isabel once again felt that tug of love inside her heart. And once again, she reminded herself that she needed to keep that love guarded and hidden, until Dillon was ready to accept it.

Dillon seemed so far away, so lost in his thoughts, she hated to bring him the news about his brother's financial woes. He had all the doors and windows flung open so that a cross breeze could blow through the wide central hallway. But his skin held a fine sheen of sweat in spite of the humid afternoon breezes roaming at will through the empty house.

He looked so lost, sitting there.

She knocked, hesitant to interrupt. How she dreaded this confrontation. But this had to be done.

"Go away," he said, not even bothering to lift his head or open his eyes. "Whoever you are, just go away."

"It's me," she called as she stepped inside the squeaky screen door.

Dillon sat up away from the wall, his eyes centering on her. "I was just thinking about you."

"Yeah, well, I've been doing some thinking myself," she replied as she stopped a short distance away from him. "I don't like being left on the dance floor, Dillon."

"I was rude," he admitted. "It's just that...you caught me totally by surprise—saying you didn't think you deserved me."

"More like I scared you away. I just want you to understand that...that I care about you, but I don't expect anything more than friendship."

"You're being honest, or at least you *think* you're being honest."

"Is it so hard for you to believe that I care?" she asked, "or are you uncomfortable *because* of my honesty? Maybe you don't think you need my help or my friendship."

He glanced away, then back up at her, his gaze shrouded. "Honesty is a tricky thing. It takes away all of our defenses." Trying to explain, he said, "I told you, I don't want to hurt you."

"Well, you did last night."

"I didn't mean to." He tilted his head, staring up at her. "You know, Isabel, I'm not going to hold you to that offer you made the other night."

"Oh, and why not?"

"I don't expect you to stay here and help me reconcile with my brother. It was sweet of you, but I'll deal with Eli on my own terms."

She tugged her hands through her hair in frustration. "In other words, mind my own business? Is that why you've been acting so erratic?"

"In other words, I don't want you to get caught in the cross fire by trying to salvage me."

Isabel moved farther into the room, then sat down on the aged planked floor, forcing him to look her in the eye. "In other words, you really don't want me around. You don't want to accept my help, right, Dillon?" When he made a move to touch her, she held up a hand. "No, I've thought about this over and over again since you walked away from me last night. You wanted just one dance, and now, we can go back to our separate lives, no hard feelings, no regrets. I get it, all right. You tease me, flirt with me, make me believe things I don't need to believe, even thrill me with a dance and a kiss or two, yet you claim you don't want me to get hurt."

She paused, swallowed back the threatening tears. "Because you don't feel the same way about me. I understand, really I do, Dillon." She turned to stare out of an open window. "Can't you see—that's exactly what I was trying to tell you last night. I'm still not good enough for a Murdock."

He reached out a hand and pulled her in his arms before she could take her next breath. "Don't," he said, his face inches from hers. "Don't ever say that to me again. Don't ever think that again."

Isabel stared at him, wishing she could read all the emotions playing across those storm-tossed eyes of his. "It's the truth, isn't it? You always did get your kicks out of torturing me—teasing, flirting, spending time with me, but never really putting forth a real commitment. I thought you and I were friends, real friends, but I was wrong about that, too, apparently.

That's the way it was when we were growing up, and that's the way it is now.''

"You are wrong," he said, his hands clutching her arms. "You are so completely off base, it's laughable."

"I'm not in a laughing mood, Dillon," she said. "And I came here for some answers."

"You won't get any from me."

She glared at him, her nose inches from his. "I'm not leaving until I do."

He let her go then. "Suit yourself." Deliberately, he turned the music louder. "I'm kinda busy here."

Isabel marched to the stereo and turned it off. "No. That silent treatment isn't going to work anymore. We need to talk."

He glanced at the stereo. "I was listening to that."

"You're going to listen to me instead."

"Oh, really? You are one stubborn woman, Issy."

"Not as stubborn as you. You danced with me last night, then left me standing there, Dillon. It's just like all those years ago, when you left without telling me goodbye. And I'm not going to let that happen ever again. Talk to me, please?"

Clearly frustrated, he threw his hands up in defeat. "About what? About my brother? About my dreams for this house?"

"That's a start, yes."

He jumped up then, waving his hands in the air. "I couldn't sleep last night, so I got this wild idea— I want to redo this house. I'm going to rebuild Wildwood, just like we talked about."

"You what?" Shocked, Isabel realized he was doing the usual, avoiding the question. "How do you think Eli will take this news?'' Maybe now would be a good time to tell him what she'd heard from Susan.

"I really don't care what my brother thinks," Dillon replied hotly. "He has his side of the road, and I have mine."

"That sure sums it up," Isabel said. "But, Dillon, about Eli—"

He didn't let her finish, let alone begin. "How much longer will you be here, anyway?"

She shrugged. "A few days. I promised Susan I'd have her proofs ready when they get back from the honeymoon."

"I'm staying a few days longer, too," he said. "I think Mama needs me here—she's exhausted after the wedding."

"Okay, but what's all this got to do with us, with you really talking to me for a change?"

Taking her by the hand, he said, "Remember when you told me I needed to learn to trust again?" At her nod, he continued, "You've taught me to trust my faith, Issy. And since the other night, since I saw what real trust is, there with you and your grandmother, I've been giving that some serious consideration. I've actually prayed about it, a lot."

"That's good. You'll need lots of faith—taking on Eli and this old house again."

He leaned close then. "Well, I have to ask you to do the same for me. Isabel, I can't tell you everything you need to know—I'm still wrestling with all of this myself. I'm asking you to trust me, to have faith in me. You did say you were willing to help me, didn't you?"

"Yes, but—"

"So will you just hang on a little longer?"

"But, Dillon, there are some things I need to tell you, today."

"And I'm telling you, no, I'm asking you, to listen to me, Isabel. If I take on this project…it will be demanding. I'll have to fight Eli, I'll have to rearrange my schedule to find time to supervise things here—"

"And that means you'll have to put our relationship on hold?"

"No, that means I'll need you more than ever."

His words, spoken with complete honesty at last, captivated her. "I don't have a problem with that, Dillon."

"But there might be some problems," he tried to explain. "Eli will make our time together miserable."

"I can deal with Eli."

"I don't want you to have to deal with Eli, and I don't want you to have to deal with all the things I've done."

She stared at him, realization dawning. "So, that's why you think you don't deserve my help, my friendship, me?"

He nodded again. "That's my excuse. For wanting to be with you, then pushing you away. For flirting with you, then being rude last night. I'm just so afraid. So afraid I'll blow it all over again."

"But, Dillon—"

"Just tell me you'll trust me, Issy. Just tell me you'll try to understand why I'm the way I am."

"I'll try," she said, resignation taking over some of her earlier determination. "I am trying. But what about Eli?"

"Right now, Eli is faraway and occupied with his

new bride. Want a tour, to see what grand plans I have for fixing this place up?"

Isabel's heart soared, then sank. She really needed to talk to him about Eli, but Dillon obviously wasn't in a listening mood. And after what he'd just told her about this house, she couldn't bring herself to shatter his hope. In a way, this might work out. If Dillon put some money back into this place, things might turn around for Eli, too.

Turning to lift her gaze up to the winding staircase, she said, "I used to bring things to your mama—sewing, laundry, fruit and vegetables that we'd been hired to pick and can, and I'd always stand in this hallway, wishing I could explore this house from top to bottom." Shrugging, she said, "Of course, I never got any farther than that old settee that used to be against that wall." She pointed to the empty spot between the parlor and the formal dining room. "Your mama would come out of one of those big rooms, all bright and dressed to the nines. She'd gush with pride and thank me for all my hard work. Then I'd hand over the finished product and hurry out the door." Her smile was bittersweet. "I'd always turn about halfway up the lane, though, just to get one more look. I thought this place was a palace."

Dillon lowered his head, his eyes falling across the hardwood floors. "It wasn't a palace at all. In fact, it wasn't much of a home. Not in the real sense of the word. It took me years to figure out my family was totally dysfunctional—make that *still* totally dysfunctional."

Surprised that he'd let her in on that obvious revelation, Isabel said, "You always seemed like the perfect family to me. I used to watch you all in church, sitting up front on your family pew. Your mother, so pretty, so fashionable, your father, so debonair, but so intimidating, like a lion ruling over his domain. And of course, you and Eli, two handsome brothers with everything good in life going for them.''

He glanced up toward the high ceiling. ''If these old walls could talk. You know, Isabel, sitting on the front row in church doesn't necessarily mean you're guaranteed a spot in Heaven. You saw a whole different picture than the real one.''

He was right, of course. Grammy also said actions spoke louder than words or appearances. And the Murdock actions spoke volumes. ''I guess so. I believe we see what we want to see.''

Tugging her along, he said, ''Well, the whole town saw what my parents *wanted* them to see, that's for sure. We kept our secrets safe and our problems behind the walls of this house. That is, until Eli and I had our parting of the way.''

Thinking he was going to open up at last, she said, ''That is when everything changed, isn't it? I guess that's why your leaving was such a shock. It was so unexpected.''

''It was a long time coming,'' he replied, a contemplative frown crossing over his features. ''My father and I...we didn't see things eye to eye, and Eli and I had our share of problems long before I took off.''

He guided her up the stairs, his big hand holding tightly to hers as he easily tried to change the tone of the conversation. ''You're gonna love these big, old rooms.''

Refusing to let him sway her from her intent, Isabel said, "I'm sure I will. But tell me, what kind of problems did you and your brother have?"

He shook his head. "Sorry, that's not part of the tour package."

Isabel watched as the wall of blankness fell back across his face, shutting her out as effectively as the shuttered windows of the upstairs landing tried to shut out the sun. Just like this old house, Dillon didn't want to give up his secrets. He would fight her every step of the way. Maybe that was what Grammy was trying to make her see. She wouldn't be fighting against Eli if she got herself involved in this; she'd be fighting against Dillon's resistance, too.

How could she tell him Eli was in trouble, when he seemed so excited about drywall and paint, when he went on and on about antiques and family heirlooms. Dillon intended to bring it all back, in full glory. But she had to wonder if he was considering restoring this house because he wanted his home back, or because he wanted the home he'd never really had. Maybe it was all a facade, and maybe he was building his dreams on that facade—the sower throwing out seeds at random, mindless of where they would land.

She'd hate to see him try to restore something that had never been there in the first place, especially when he could easily lose it all again. If things had been as bad as he'd indicated, he was definitely sowing on ground that had not been as solid as everyone believed.

They finished the tour—five bedrooms, an upstairs sitting area and den, four bathrooms, and then back

down the stairs to the central hallway with four huge
open rooms on each side. There was an office just
opposite of the long kitchen. Dillon had made that
into his own temporary living quarters.

Within each room, he'd talked about what he hoped
to accomplish. Restoring his great-grandmother's
four-poster rice bed, the one that had been especially
designed for her up in New England, which now
stood empty and open, without even a feather mat-
tress to grace its frames, finding antiques to match the
ones Eli had sold off or given away, bringing this
house back to life in a timeless fashion with respected
memories and traditional treasures, both bought and
borrowed—he was willing to put everything into
making this house what he pictured in his mind.

Even though she knew she should, Isabel couldn't
find it in her heart to bring up Eli's problems.

"Restoring this place will be a huge task," she said
as they moved back down the stairs. "But you seem
to know what you're talking about—antiques and
heirlooms! I always remembered you as being only
interested in fast cars."

He shook his head. "I was young, a rebel in the
worst way. I've learned a lot since then." He gave
her a look that touched her heart, yet revealed nothing. "I know what really matters now, Isabel."

His words and the look in his eyes caused her
breath to flutter much in the same way as the faded
lace curtains at a nearby floor-to-ceiling window.

"Such as this house, and rebuilding your life
here," she said to deflect the warm sensations pouring
over her. She had to remind herself he could never
love her the way she loved him, no matter how he

looked at her. She had to remember what really did matter the most to Dillon Murdock. "It should turn out beautifully," she told him. "I hope it does."

The intimacy was gone, replaced by that controlled, brooding mask...and doubt. "You don't sound so sure."

"It just seems like a huge undertaking for someone who didn't want to stick around."

"You don't believe I have sticking power?"

She stood on the last step of the curving stairs, with him down below her. Looking down at him, she prayed he did see this old house restored, and she prayed even harder that he'd find the restoration his tattered soul needed. "I believe in *you,* Dillon. I told you that. But I really wish you'd talk to Eli, try to patch things up before you spring this on him."

"And I told you, I'm not worried about Eli—except to protect you from him. I won't let him ruin what we have between us."

"Why would he even try? I mean, I know he's never liked me—he thinks I'm just some poor country girl. But, I'm not that girl anymore. I can stand up to Eli. And I will, just to prove to you that I'm stronger now."

Dillon looked over at her, forcing the old blankness to take over his expression and his emotions. He couldn't let her see the truth there in his eyes. He refused to open her up to that kind of pain. She might be stronger now, but in some ways she was still fragile. What they had together now, friendship or more, was too precious to him to squander in another fight with Eli. If she knew, if she even suspected, that he and Eli had quarreled about her and her family all

162 *Wedding At Wildwood*

those years ago, she'd bolt like a fawn and he'd never see her again.

Remembering all the old hurts Eli had inflicted on him, remembering his brother's dire warnings and malicious jeers, Dillon steeled his heart against loving Isabel. He didn't want to bring her into his family; she'd only wind up resenting him for loving her, for making her love him. Theirs could never be an easy coupling. Eli would make sure of that, just as he had once before. And no amount of praying or repentance could help this situation.

"Dillon?"

He heard the need in her voice, saw the hurt and confusion in her eyes. By trying to protect her, he was hurting her just as badly. Thinking he should just grab her by the hand and run away with her, Dillon shook his head. He was tired of running. And he was also tired of fighting his feelings for Isabel. He was no longer content with having her assume the worst of him. So he did the only thing he could do. He gave up.

"You want the truth, Issy?" he said now, his heart crystallizing and breaking like the aged paint on the walls. "You want to know what makes me the way I am?"

"I want you to be honest with me."

Coming close, he willed himself to find the strength to let her know his real feelings. "Okay, I'll tell you, but you might not like it."

Shaking her head, she said, "What do you mean?"

The war inside him shifting into a gentle surrender, he pulled her into his arms. "I mean, I think I'm falling for you. And I don't want that to happen, not yet. Not here on Wildwood. Maybe when we both get back to our own worlds, away from here, maybe I can think straight about all of this. You offer me friendship and support, but by doing that, you don't know what you're asking in return. I might not be able to give you everything you need in return.''

Filled with shock and joy at the same time, Isabel touched a hand to his face. ''What if I told you I feel the same way—about the falling for you part, I mean.''

He swallowed, stared at her, touched a hand to her hair. ''I'd say what I've already said—I don't deserve you.''

''Okay,'' she said at last. ''I'm sorry. I'm sorry I threw myself at you, sorry I forced you to care about me. I'm sorry I've been hovering around…as Eli put it…chasing after you.''

He lifted his head then, his eyes flashing fire. ''Eli? What did he say to you?''

Her head down, she whispered, ''He told me you'd never settle for one woman. He told me you'd never change.''

A frustrated rage simmered beneath the deliberate calm Dillon tried so hard to maintain. ''That's my big brother. He always did have me pegged.''

Tossing her hair back, Isabel gave him a pleading look. ''Well, this time, he was wrong, *wasn't* he? You say you might be in love with me, yet you tell me you don't want to love me—you're afraid of something. You're hiding something deep inside. And you won't let me in. That hurts much worse than anything Eli could ever do to me. Much worse.''

She didn't have to convince him. He could see the

hurt in her beautiful eyes, in her defeated stance, in the frown marring her expression. But this hurt would go away; if he told her everything, it would be ten times worse.

"I'm truly sorry, Isabel," he managed to say. "But some habits die hard. I'm not very good at talking things out, and until you came along, I didn't think I was capable of loving anyone. It's scaring me."

Hearing the sound of tires on gravel and clay, Dillon pulled his gaze away from her to look out the open double doors at the front of the house. "We've got company."

Struggling somewhere between resentment and rejoicing, Isabel watched as Dillon headed up the hallway to see who'd come up the drive, then she took the time to get herself together.

Dillon loved her, but he didn't want to love her. Something was holding him back—maybe his own fear of making that final commitment, maybe his problems with his family, maybe their life-styles being too different, and too far apart. Whatever it was, Dillon still didn't trust her enough to tell her about it.

"Just leave," she told herself now. "Just tell him about his brother, then go before things get much, much worse."

But she'd waited too late. With Dillon's next heated words to the man out in his yard, things went from bad to worse in a matter of minutes. Rushing up the long, wide hallway, Isabel heard his shouts as she reached the front doors.

"I won't let you do this. I won't let Eli do this!"

Isabel hurried out onto the porch to see what the

two men were arguing about, but the sign in Leland Burke's hand told her everything she needed to know.

The Wildwood mansion and the surrounding land, was going to be put up for public auction, one week from today.

Dillon was going to lose the home he loved so much, the home he'd come back to, the home he had just decided to rebuild. And now, it was too late for Isabel to warn him, or to help him.

And it was too late for her to tell him that she'd known for days now that something like this might happen.

Chapter Eleven

"**M**other, you have to tell me what's going on!"

Dillon watched his mother's face, saw the confusion and shock that had changed her usually serene features into a mask of grief. It wasn't easy interrogating his mother this way, but someone had to explain why his brother would be willing to let the bank auction off part of Wildwood—the main part of Wildwood as far as Dillon was concerned.

Cynthia seemed to age right before his eyes. Swallowing back some of the rage he'd felt at seeing Leland Burke in his yard just over an hour ago, Dillon took a long breath then reached out a hand to take his mother's trembling fingers. "What's Eli done, Mother?"

"I honestly don't understand," Cynthia said weakly. "I just can't believe he'd stand for this—auctioning off the plantation house. Why, it's ridiculous to even think of such a thing."

"The sign's up on the front field, Mother," Dillon

reminded her. "I yanked it down, but Leland put it back up. According to him, Eli mortgaged that piece of property and now the mortgage is due. We'll lose it, Mama. We'll lose Wildwood. From the sound of things, we've already lost it."

Cynthia shook her head, disbelief evident in her misty eyes. "That house is over 150 years old. I shouldn't ever have left that old place."

Dillon tilted his head, his voice softening. "I know, Mama. I know. We should have taken better care. *I* should have taken better care of the place."

"I never wanted to move, you know," Cynthia said, her voice low and raspy. "I begged Eli to let me stay there. I wanted to live out my days in that old house—you know how I love my wildflowers. But he insisted I'd be more comfortable here with him."

"Why did you move in here if you knew you wouldn't be happy?" Dillon asked now, concern for his mother calming his earlier anger. He could understand Eli wanting to punish him, but it was cruel to do this to their mother.

Cynthia held his hand in hers, her eyes bright with tears. "I didn't want to be alone, and Eli insisted it would be easier on both of us. I didn't argue very much, because I missed your father so terribly, and you—oh, Dillon, how I longed for you to come home and make peace with your brother. I prayed for it and when you came back, I thought my prayers would be answered." She hushed, looked over at him, then reached up a hand to touch the spike of inky hair covering his forehead. "But now, it looks like that won't be possible. I can't believe we might actually have to give up Wildwood.''

"Not if I can help it," Dillon said, letting go of her hand to pace the length of the kitchen. "I might not be able to make peace with Eli, but I certainly don't intend to stand by and watch him destroy Wildwood." Whirling, he glared out the window at the sign now back on the grass in front of the old mansion. "I'll do whatever I have to, to save that piece of land."

"It'll be another fight," Cynthia said. "I don't know if I can stand this."

Dillon shot a hand through his hair, then looked at his mother. "I don't want another fight, but I won't run away this time, Mama. I came home hoping to find forgiveness and a fresh start with Eli, but since I've been here, he's done nothing but ridicule me and condemn me—it's not ever going to change." He turned back to the window, his mind made up.

"Well, I might as well live up to my reputation. If he wants a battle, I'll give him one. I'm older now, and stronger, and I won't let him do this to our family."

Cynthia leaned her elbows on the table, then placed her head in her hands. "How can you stop this? I had no idea Eli had done this—mortgaging our land. Why, we've never owed a dime to that bank—we helped build that bank with our hard-earned money and our backing. How can Leland even be a party to something like this?"

"Leland is well within his rights," Dillon explained. "He wouldn't give me all the details, but apparently Eli is heavily in debt to the Wildwood

Bank and Trust. I intend to find out exactly what my brother's been up to. Starting right now.''

"What are you going to do?" Cynthia asked.

Dillon headed up the hallway toward Eli's elegant office and all the files and documents concerning the operation of Wildwood. "I'm going to do a little research—find out just how much money your elder son owes to the bank.''

"Debt," Cynthia repeated, her mouth falling open. "We won't be able to hold our heads up in public. I'll be ashamed to walk down the street. Your father would turn over in his grave.''

Dillon didn't reply. Answering to the fickle citizens of Wildwood was the least of his worries since he'd had plenty enough practice at that particular chore. But he hated seeing his mother this way. He didn't care what others thought of him or his brother, but Cynthia would have a hard time dealing with the public condemnation and scorn.

Theirs was one of the founding families of this town—the town had been named after the plantation. Wildwood, the town, was just an extension of the Murdock dynasty that had started with cotton long before the Civil War. This land had survived that war, and had continued to thrive and prosper with other crops and other ventures. Farming was in the Murdock blood. Which made it that much harder to accept what Eli had done.

Cynthia was used to everything being taken care of, everything tidy and in its place. She'd never had to deal with very much scandal. Dillon wanted to comfort her, but right now he was too anxious to find out all the sordid details of Eli's business ventures.

"You should call our lawyer," Cynthia suggested, her head popping up. "Fletcher Curtis will know what to do, since I certainly don't."

Dillon didn't trust the family lawyer enough to call him right now as Fletcher had been the other man standing with Eli and Leland yesterday morning. Well, he'd deal with all of those involved later. Now, he'd call Sanford—see if there was any way his business manager could arrange for Dillon to pay off the mortgage on Wildwood.

If he'd been more alert, Dillon thought, he could have tried to stop this sooner. But no, he'd been too caught up in his feelings for Isabel, too preoccupied with her honesty and his denial to notice anything out of the ordinary around here. And Eli had covered his tracks very well, apparently.

Now, he stomped up the hall, thinking his mother was right about one thing. Murdocks didn't fall into debt. They often bailed other people out of debt. Other people usually owed the Murdocks money. Isabel's own father, Leonard, had come to Roy Murdock, asking for a loan once. But Dillon didn't want to think of that fateful day right now, or what it had cost both him and Isabel.

Thoughts of Isabel reminded Dillon of how they'd left things earlier. After he'd practically attacked Leland in the front yard, Isabel had rushed out of the house, her face ashen, her eyes wide with shock and...and something else he couldn't quite put his finger on. Too distracted by this latest development, though, he'd ignored her to try to pin Leland down on the details of this upcoming auction.

After arguing with the man until they'd both lost

their tempers, Dillon had turned to see Isabel walking away, back toward her grandmother's house. Humiliated, and beyond reason, he'd let her go. What could he say to her now? How could he explain that he loved her so much it hurt with each breath he took, but that his family problems had once again gotten in the way of that love?

He'd go to her later and explain. He had just found her again—he wouldn't lose her now. His priority had to be saving Wildwood, and that meant concentrating on getting to the bottom of Eli's deceptions. Slinging his body down in Eli's burgundy leather office chair, Dillon clicked on the computer sitting on one corner of the executive-style desk. While he waited for the computer to boot up, he looked out the window, toward the little cottage where Isabel had spent her childhood.

Leonard Landry had spent his entire adult life on that little spot of land. Isabel's father had come to work for the Murdocks as a teenager, then continued working here after marrying Isabel's quiet, shy mother, Miriam. How could a man make that kind of sacrifice? How could he continue taking orders from someone else without some sort of resentment building up inside him?

Well, the resentment had been there, all right. But not in Leonard Landry. The resentment had become Isabel's legacy. It was now so deeply embedded inside her, Dillon doubted she herself even recognized it for what it really was. Which was why Dillon still found it hard to believe that she could possibly love him. She didn't know how much he loved her, and how hard he'd fought for her all those years ago. He'd

fought then, and he'd lost. And he'd failed Isabel's
family.

But Mr. Landry had accepted his lot in life and had
worked as hard as any man could, trying to keep his
family out of debt. And he'd done it on the meager
wages Dillon's father paid out, without ever once
questioning or demanding any changes.

Except for that one time.

Memories of that day and the horrible consequences of Dillon's interference came back to him
now, capturing him like the blinking cursor light on
the humming computer screen. Isabel was right; that
was when everything had changed.

He wouldn't hurt Isabel with the ugliness of his
father and brother's snobbery and prejudice. She'd
never be able to face him again if she knew all about
that terrible day so long ago.

Well, I won't lose you again, Issy, he thought now
as he grimly started scrolling Eli's files, *and I won't
lose Wildwood.* This was his opportunity to make
things up to his mother, and he intended to take full
advantage of it.

When this was all over, he'd tell Isabel everything.
He prayed that she'd understand and not turn away
in disgust. And he prayed for guidance; he needed
God's help with this, and he hoped that the good Lord
would give a sinner like him one more chance.

Since sleep was impossible, Isabel worked long
into the night, developing roll after roll of film and
several sheets of proof shots from the hundreds of
pictures she'd taken since coming back to Wildwood.
Most were of the wedding and the activities leading

up to that event, but a lot of the pictures she now held in her hands were of Wildwood itself...and Dillon.

At least she'd have these memories to take back to Savannah with her. She'd have her own private album of their time together here on this land. It would have to be enough, she decided. Because Dillon had more important things on his mind now. His home was in jeopardy; he didn't have time to spend with a woman who'd never measure up to the Murdock standards.

Remembering how angry he'd been earlier that day, remembering her part in all of this, Isabel shook her head. Why hadn't she prepared Dillon for this? Why had she held back the information Susan had given her? If she'd gone to Dillon sooner, he might have confronted Eli before that auction sign had gone up. Now, Dillon was madder than ever and in shock over this latest turn of events.

Had Eli deliberately waited until after the wedding to drop this little bombshell? Why couldn't he have at least told Dillon what to expect. Because he probably thought Dillon would be long gone before the sign went up. Boy, would he be in for a surprise when he returned from his honeymoon and found Dillon still here and fighting harder than ever to keep his home.

Isabel leaned back in her chair by the window, wishing she'd had the courage to help Dillon. But she'd waited too long, hoping he'd trust her enough to share his past miseries with her.

"It was just wistful thinking, Lord," she said into the still summer night. "Just me being foolish again."

Her mother used to tell her not to wish too hard for things she could never have.

"You can't just go out and start snapping pictures and call yourself a photographer, honey. Best you get a job at the sewing factory in town and bring home an honest day's wages," her mother had told her years ago.

Well, she'd tried that, Isabel remembered now. It hadn't lasted because she couldn't conform to the work the way so many women living in the rural areas had. She wanted an honest day's work, but she also wanted more.

"No, Mama, I had to go out to prove you all wrong, didn't I?"

She'd enrolled at the local community college about thirty miles away from Wildwood, much to the dismay of her parents.

"Girls don't need that kind of education," her father had warned. "You just need to find a good man and settle down. How you gonna get back and forth to that fancy school anyway?"

Isabel had found a way. She'd worked at the sewing factory just long enough to buy a run-down used car. And she'd driven that car back and forth for two years, using the scholarship she'd earned through the help of a guidance counselor at Wildwood High to help pay her tuition.

Then, a few days after she'd graduated, two years after Dillon had left Wildwood, she'd told her parents she was moving away.

"And where do you think you're going?" her bewildered father had asked.

"I've found a job in Valdosta," she'd explained, afraid that they'd talk her right out of moving to the larger town a few miles north, if she gave them time to argue with her. "I'll be working for a newspaper there, as a secretary. I'll be able to take a few photographs here and there—"

"She's crazy," Leonard had told her mother. "Crazy, just plain crazy. Girls don't run off to Valdosta to work for a newspaper."

But this girl had. And from there, she'd transferred to Savannah and now, she was independent and stable, on her own and...still trying to prove herself.

Funny, when she looked back on things, she'd always thought she'd find Dillon somewhere out there. Isabel had never dreamed she'd have to return to Wildwood to find the one man she would always love.

Well, finding him was one thing. Spending the rest of her life with him was quite another. She'd waited; she'd tried to talk to him, to get him to talk to her. She'd come so close to telling him about Eli's problems.

And she'd failed at all those attempts.

Now, Dillon had a new battle to fight. And he didn't need her right in the thick of things. She'd just be a distraction now, no matter how willing she was to stay here and see him through this.

And yet, she couldn't just leave.

"You told me I wasn't very good at waiting, Grammy," she said now as she touched a finger to the first picture she'd taken of Dillon. Holding the black-and-white photograph close, she said, "Lord, I've been waiting most of my life for this man. I've prayed about this, longed for him to love me back— at times I didn't even know or understand what I was waiting for. Now, I do." She closed her eyes, the sweet memory of Dillon's kisses causing her to draw in her breath. "I thank You for bringing me home again, for letting me see that Dillon means so much to me, and he always will. I guess I'm going to have to leave it in Your hands from now on. We need Your help, Lord."

She'd finish the preliminary photographs of the wedding. She'd have everything in order for Susan so the bride could pick the best shots for her wedding album. Then Isabel could concentrate on Dillon.

Holding Dillon's picture away so that she could barely make out his features in the soft light from a nearby lamp, she whispered, "I made you a promise. I'll see it through."

When he'd left all those years ago, she'd been hurt that he hadn't told her goodbye.

This time, she wouldn't be able to tell him goodbye.

"He asked me to trust him," she reminded herself again as she turned out all the lights but one and sat there clutching Dillon's image close to her heart. "And that's what I intend to do."

From his spot in Eli's office, Dillon saw one soft yellow light burning in the Landry house down the road. It was late, so late, and everything about the countryside was quiet and still. Shadows loomed here and there, waiting, hushed, warm with the wind of a summer night. The sleeping land reached out to him, holding him close in its embrace.

His land.

Isabel's land.

They'd lived here, watched this land change and grow, shift and blossom. Apart, they'd lived a life together that few people could ever understand. And tonight, they'd each worked at their individual tasks, in individual, completely different homes. That, at least, brought Dillon some measure of comfort. Somehow, he knew Isabel was there in the dark, thinking of things, thinking of him maybe, just as he was thinking of things, and her, always her.

He sank back against the soft leather of the office chair, picturing Isabel hard at work in her makeshift darkroom, her green eyes bright with excitement and pride as she created her own special way with film and chemicals.

Dillon smiled now, proud of her gift, proud that she'd overcome all the obstacles holding her back, to move on with her life. She could have easily settled for living out her days in Wildwood, Georgia, but she'd had the courage to follow her heart.

He wished he had that kind of courage. Instead, he'd been a coward who'd run away from his home and his responsibilities. He'd followed nothing except his own stubborn pride, and he'd wasted so many years and so much time holding on to a grudge that didn't seem to matter very much right now.

As angry as he was with his brother, Dillon also felt some sympathy for Eli. With Dillon's defection and later, their father's death, Eli had been left with the tremendous responsibility of running the huge plantation. He'd done the best he could, under the circumstances. Granted, according to the files in front of him, Eli had made some bad decisions, but then he'd had no help, none at all.

Running his hands through his hair, Dillon fought exhaustion and regret. If he'd stayed here, this might not be happening now. If he'd stayed here, he and Isabel might have wound up together. But no, her life had turned out much better without him. He had to remember that, at least. She didn't have to deal with the mess he would have to face come morning. And he intended to keep her out of it, for her own sake.

His brother had really created a monster of tangled finances and bad business decisions. Apparently, Eli had a dream of reopening the old, long-idle cotton gin that had once been the mainstay of Wildwood. But before his brother had accomplished that particular feat, Eli had decided he needed a new house and a new car and new farm equipment.

In essence, his brother had robbed Peter to pay Paul.

In essence, not only the old plantation house, but most of the Wildwood land, was in danger of being sold or auctioned off. From everything he'd been able to decipher in the computer files, Dillon now understood that things were worse, much worse than anyone knew, probably even Eli himself.

With a groan of frustration, Dillon hung his head. He sat there, adding and subtracting, reworking the figures, trying to come up with a viable solution, trying to understand what had driven Eli to such extremes, but nothing worked.

Yet he would not give up. And in the back of his mind, a solution had started to form, a germ of an idea that was swiftly growing into the only way out of this whole ordeal. If Eli would go for it.

Tired, Dillon decided he'd go back to Wildwood and try to get some sleep. As he reached to turn off the single lamp splattering bright light across the cluttered desk, his hand struck a worn Bible sitting off to the side, on top of some battered, stuffed folders.

His father's Bible. Did Eli actually read the word of God?

Curious, Dillon picked up the leather-bound book and surveyed it. When was the last time he'd actually taken the time to read the Bible? When was the last time he'd turned to God, really turned to God, for help in his life?

He remembered a time when God was his only salvation, when he'd had no hope left and he'd reached out into the dark night. He'd found his salvation then, alone and lonely, and on his last shreds of dignity.

Would God listen to him one more time?

Without hesitation, Dillon opened the book to a passage that Eli had obviously marked with a torn piece of paper.

It was the book of Ecclesiastes. The first chapter was headed ''The Vanity of Life.''

Shocked, and even more curious, Dillon started reading.

"Vanity of vanities," said the Preacher; "Vanity of vanities, all is vanity."

"What profit has a man from all his labor, in which he toils under the sun? One generation passes away, and another generation comes; but the earth abides forever."

The earth abides forever. This land had survived in spite of everything that had happened. The winds of both fortune and bad luck had blown over Wildwood, and still this earth had withstood the test of time.

"What were you searching for, there in those passages, Eli?" Dillon wondered now. "Did you realize too late that you'd overstepped your bounds, that your vanity had cost you more than you were willing to pay?"

Dillon got up, placed the Bible back where he'd found it, then on second thought, picked it back up and clutched it underneath his arm. He had a lot of soul-searching to do and this particular book might help him find some of the answers he needed.

For the first time in many years, Dillon's heart went out to his older brother. How long had Eli carried the burdens of Wildwood on his shoulders, without any support or understanding, without any guidance, except what he could find in this worn book?

"I've been unfair to you, brother," Dillon whispered as he closed the kitchen door and walked through the gardens toward home.

He was still bitter, but he felt a new peace settling over the earlier fatigue that racked his body. He would try, really try, to understand why Eli had done the things he'd done.

And, he'd offer his help to his brother.

Holding the thick, worn Bible close, Dillon stared up at the house he loved so much. And he prayed his stubborn brother would be able to accept his help.

Together, they could keep this land.

Together, they too could abide forever.

Chapter Twelve

Dillon hesitated a few seconds, then knocked softly on the heavy wooden door of the Landry house. The information he had to tell Isabel and her grandmother weighed heavily in the pit of his stomach, choking him with a helpless despair. Better coming from him, though, than through official papers from the bank.

Martha opened the door and smiled brightly. "Dillon, what brings you to my doorstep on a humid Monday morning?"

"Hello, Mrs. Landry," he began, shifting his booted feet in an uncomfortable fidget. "I...I need to talk to you."

"Sure, c'mon in," Martha replied, swinging an arm in invitation. "How about a cup of coffee and some apple cake?"

"Coffee sounds good," he said as he entered the small dining room. "I'll pass on the cake. I'm not very hungry, but thanks anyway."

"Suit yourself." Martha indicated a chair, then

turned to go into the kitchen for his coffee. "Isabel, as you might remember, has a rather large sweet tooth, so I always bake on the rare occasions she comes home. How that girl gets away with eating all that fattening stuff is beyond me. Guess she walks it all off, out on her photography excursions. She does have a talent for taking pictures, doesn't she?"

"Yes, ma'am." Dillon let Martha's proud chatter pour over him like a soothing balm. She didn't have to brag to him about her granddaughter. He was completely convinced of how special Isabel was. Which made his visit all the more difficult.

"Where is Isabel?" he asked now, glancing around after Martha handed him a steaming mug of coffee.

Martha gave him an indulgent look. "She's on the phone in the bedroom, talking to her agent. She was up to the wee hours again last night, working on those wedding layouts. Wants to get them in order, so she can have a few days to concentrate on...other things."

Dillon slammed his cup down, his head coming up. "She's not leaving, is she?"

Martha placed her hands on the back of her own chair. "I honestly don't know what her plans are. But she will eventually have to get back to Savannah, of course."

Worried, Dillon said, "She didn't mention anything about a new assignment—I thought she'd be staying a while. But then, I've been a bit preoccupied since the wedding."

Martha sat down, then patted his hand, a look of tenderness entering her eyes. "I sure am sorry it all had to come to this. Imagine, Wildwood being sold at auction.''

''Yeah, it's a raw deal.'' Dillon willed himself not to panic. Right now, he didn't really care so much about Wildwood. Surely, Isabel wasn't planning to leave yet?

He glanced at Martha, saw the sympathy in her eyes. It wouldn't take much more of her grandmotherly persuasion before he'd fall into the woman's arms like a baby and babble out all his fears and frustrations, namely that he was about to lose both his home and the woman he loved.

This was supposed to have been simple, he thought, his bitterness coming back to provide a nice warm cloak that effectively blocked out Martha's caring attitude. He should have been the same old cynical Dillon Murdock, well on his way back to Atlanta by now. But he was no longer that man.

Now, he was having to deal with all these new emotions, such as panic and pain, and a fierce need to go grab the phone away from Isabel and tell her agent to get lost.

''Why don't you relax, son?'' Martha said as she refreshed his coffee.

''I can't,'' he quipped. ''I'm a Murdock, remember? We have a hard time dealing with the truth.''

''And the truth is?'' Martha asked gently.

''I don't want her to leave,'' he blurted out. And immediately turned red with embarrassment at the admission.

But from the look of understanding and concern in Martha's eyes to the warmth of her hand covering his, Dillon knew he could tell this woman anything and she would neither condemn him nor judge him. Martha Landry was not self-righteous or full of overblown pride.

And she proved it with her next statement. "See there, that wasn't so bad, now, was it?"

He had to smile then. "No, I guess not." And he did relax, in spite of the news he had to tell them. Then he started talking. "You know, Mrs. Landry, I've never had this kind of stability, this kind of honesty in my life. In fact, my family's ability to hide the truth has been a carefully calculated form of denial. And the worst sort of hypocrisy."

"Because you all smoothed things over?"

He nodded. "Behind closed doors, that's where the real show started—the condemnation, the name-calling and the badges of shame, the humiliation of knowing I'd never be able to live up to Murdock standards—and Eli was usually the master of ceremonies."

Martha looked thoughtful. "Well, now *he's* going to be the brunt of scandal and rumors and condemnation."

Dillon took a sip of coffee, then lowered his head. "Yes, and at one time, I would have relished that. But now, it doesn't bring me any pleasure or peace. Instead, it makes me sick to my stomach."

"You look defeated, son," Martha said, giving him another gentle pat. "Is it as bad as it sounds?"

"Worse," he replied, impatient to get this part of the ugliness over. Taking a deep breath, he gave Martha a direct look. "Which is why I came by. I really need to talk to both you and Isabel."

"About what?" Isabel said as she entered the

room, clearly surprised to find Dillon sitting at her kitchen table.

Dillon stood up, a worried expression on his face. "Hi."

"Hi," she replied. "You don't look too hot."

"I don't feel too hot," he admitted as he slumped back in his chair. And he gained no satisfaction from noting the dark circles underneath her eyes. Although she looked as lovely as ever in her sleeveless khaki ankle-length shirtdress, with her long hair still damp and unruly from her shower, he could tell that she, too, had had another rough night.

Isabel watched him watching her. Unable to take the heat from his eyes, or the feeling being in the same room with him brought over her, she tried to stay rational. But he obviously had more bad news. Heading straight for the coffeepot, she asked over her shoulder, "Did you find out anything else about the auction?"

Dillon waited for her to join Martha and him at the table. "More than I want to know." Rubbing a hand over his unshaven face, he sent Isabel a beseeching look. "My brother has gone and got himself in one big mess."

Martha automatically handed Isabel a fat slice of warm brown apple cake. "Eat something, honey." Then, turning back to Dillon, she asked, "Is he really going to let the bank auction off part of Wildwood?"

Dillon looked down at his near empty coffee cup. "He doesn't have any choice. Technically, the bank now owns the land, since he defaulted on the loan they issued a few years back. If Leland doesn't get a good bid from the auction, he'll just slap a For Sale sign up and get rid of it that way.''

"But the auction's quicker," Martha stated, nodding her understanding.

"Yep." Dillon drummed his fingers on the table, his eyes never leaving Isabel's face. "I've gone over the books—took half the day and night just trying to decipher what all Eli *has* done. My brother's record-keeping is haphazard at best. I can't seem to find the title to this place."

Isabel's heart went out to Dillon. She could tell this was killing him inside. All his hopes had been dashed with a cruelty that must have felt like another slap in the face from his cold, condemning brother. Feeling guilt all the way to her soul for not at least warning Dillon about Eli's problems, she had to look away from his sharp, unrelenting gaze. She couldn't face him this morning. Especially when she knew he'd be so hurt and angry if he found out she'd kept this from him.

Changing the subject with lightning swift accuracy, Dillon gave her a pointed look. "Are you leaving, Issy?"

Looking up, Isabel ignored the knowing expression on her grandmother's quizzical face. Nervous, she rammed a fork into the aromatic cake sitting in front of her. Not that she was hungry, but she had to at least look natural and unaffected. "I called in to check with my agent about any upcoming bookings, and I've been offered a lucrative assignment from a southern lifestyle magazine. They want me to do some work on a few tourist spots around Georgia. The magazine's based in Atlanta and I'll have to go there to meet with the editors, but—''

She stopped as Dillon's dark brows shot up like twin question marks. ''Oh, yeah? Well, I guess you have to do what you have to do, right?'' Before she could explain, he rushed on. ''I understand. I have a business to run myself. Luckily, I've got very capable managers holding down the fort, but sooner or later, I'll have to make a quick trip back to Atlanta.'' As if he were talking to himself, he added, ''And there's really no reason for you to stay here any longer, right?''

Isabel glanced at her grandmother and saw the questioning expression on Martha's face. Dillon thought she was leaving. And he didn't want her to go. Touched, she sat there looking across at his handsome, confused face.

But when she tried to speak, he only held up a hand. ''Before you go, I think you ought to know something.''

''Oh?'' She gave him a look that spoke of both hope and regret. ''What's that, Dillon?''

Dillon willed his drumming fingers to a shaky quiet. Then, glancing from Isabel's questioning eyes to her grandmother's curious stare, he said, ''Well, there's no easy way to say this, but...it's about the auction.''

''What?'' Isabel said.

Dillon let out a defeated sigh. ''The auction includes the plantation house, of course, and about fifty surrounding acres of land.''

''The wildflower field,'' Isabel said, the sick feeling in her gut growing worse by the minute. Well, Eli might not have wanted the auction, but he'd be getting his revenge, anyway. If he couldn't wipe away the wildflowers with a mower, he'd watch them become trampled by the highest bidder.

"Yes, that, too." Dillon sat up, ran a hand through the straight, shiny locks mashed against his forehead, then plunged ahead. "And, well, it also includes something else—"

"This house," Isabel finished, her anguished gaze slowly lifting to his face.

Dillon nodded his head, his hand reaching across the table to grasp hers. "Yes, Isabel. The bank is going to auction off your home as part of the package." Giving Martha an apologetic glance, he added, "Leland tells me that once that happens, you'll have about thirty days to vacate the premises."

Isabel stomped up the path that wound through the wildflower field, with Dillon hot on her trail. "How could Eli let this happen? How, Dillon?"

Not waiting for a response, she paced back and forth, her eyes moving over the serene yellow faces of black-eyed Susans and the lush carpeting of blue phlox. Even the flowers looked wilted and dejected today, their fate sealed right along with Isabel's.

"I can't believe this is happening! What has my grandmother ever done to deserve this? She's worked for your family most of her life, and now this?"

"Isabel, stop," Dillon said as he stood in front of her to halt her pacing. When she tried to step around him, he reached his arms out to grab hold of her shoulders. "Stop."

"I can't stop," she shouted, her eyes bright with

bitter tears that she refused to let fall. "I've got to do something to help my grandmother. Dillon, she has no other place to go. She's lived in that house since my grandfather died over twenty years ago, since my parents died. I just can't—"

Dillon pulled her into his arms. "I know and I'm sorry. And I promise you this—I'm going to fight this with every breath in my body."

Isabel fell against him, drained and defeated. "I can't believe Eli has let it come to this."

Dillon patted a hand on her lush hair, then kissed the top of her head. "I intend to question him on it, believe me."

Pulling away, Isabel gave him a scrutinizing glare. "And what can you do, other than fight with him again? He wanted both of us gone, and now, because of his greed and mismanagement, my grandmother will have to leave, too."

Dillon held her by her arms, forcing her to listen to him. "I intend to do plenty. I've racked my brain all night and half the morning about this, and I've come up with some options."

She lifted her chin, her eyes widening. "Such as?"

"I'd rather not discuss it just yet. I want to talk to Eli first."

Pushing his hands away, she said, "Fine. That's just fine. You still can't trust me enough to level with me, can you, Dillon?"

"What?" He placed a hand on her bare arm, tugging her back around to face him. "What's that supposed to mean, anyway?"

Isabel gave him an openmouthed look of disbelief. "Isn't it obvious? You aren't ready to tell me how we're supposed to get out of this mess? How can I possibly stay calm when I don't even know what's going to happen to my grandmother? Why can't you just trust me and let me help you?"

Dillon plopped down on the ground, mindless of the buzzing bees and colorful butterflies he'd startled away from the fragrant flowers. "It's not about trust, Isabel. I'm trying to keep you out of this. You shouldn't have to be involved in the ugly dealings of the Murdock clan."

Glaring down at him, she said, "But I am involved. I'm involved all the way around. I'm involved because of my grandmother, I'm involved because I came back here in the first place, and I'm especially involved because of…because of—"

"Because of me," he finished just as he lifted a hand to pull her down beside him, his expression daring her to try and get away.

No, she wanted to shout, *because of my own stupidity. Because I didn't listen to Susan and tell you the truth.* Dillon thought this was all his fault, but he was so wrong. And now, she didn't know how to be honest with him. She was so afraid she'd lose him forever.

So she stayed silent, then fell down on the soft cushion of flowers, scaring a pair of squawking blue jays out of a nearby camellia bush.

"I tried to warn you," he said on a low, husky voice. "I tried to tell you that I'd only bring you misery."

"*You* didn't do this," she retorted, her fingers busy plucking the petals off of an already crushed variegated petunia. *And I tried to warn you, but not in time.*

Dillon turned to her then, his eyes centering on her face, his expression softening with a tenderness that took her by surprise. "Stay here, Issy," he said, his voice low and vulnerable. "I'm not good at asking for help, but I could use yours right now."

Isabel shut her eyes, then sent up a quick prayer. He wouldn't want her help anymore if he knew the truth. But she could at least tell him that she'd never intended on leaving in the first place. "I am staying, Dillon," she said, her hand on his arm. "I turned down the assignment in Atlanta."

Dillon covered her hand with his own, then pressed it against his face, closing his eyes in apparent relief. "I thought—"

"You thought wrong," she whispered, tears pricking her eyes. "I told you I'd stay and I intend to do just that. Besides, I can't leave my grandmother now, can I?"

"No." He wrapped his other arm around her neck. "I shouldn't ask this of you, I know that. I should send you packing, get you away from this mess. But I'm being selfish—I don't want you to go."

Trying to be rational in spite of his lips grazing the palm of her hand, she said, "I'll probably just make things worse. I'm so angry right now, it's hard not to lash out at Eli."

"You let me take care of Eli," Dillon stated, the tenderness in his words and his gentle actions melting her fear and guilt. But she also sensed something else there. A warning?

Lifting her hand away, Isabel stared him down. "Just exactly how do you plan on doing that?"

He shrugged. "I'm learning patience, and I'm trying hard to forgive him. But...this isn't going to be easy.''

Isabel sighed and hugged him close. "No, it's not. And I guess I need to get back inside and help Grammy decide what her options are. There aren't that many available houses around here, and she's on a fixed income. And I doubt she'd be willing to move to my cramped apartment in Savannah.''

"She's lucky to have you for a granddaughter," he told her, pride shining in his eyes.

"And what about you, Dillon?" If he wouldn't say it, she'd say it for him. "You say you could use my help, but do you need me here?"

Dillon sank back against the soft perfume of a thousand flowers, his heart thumping quicker than the spindly green grasshopper escaping across the denim covering his leg. What was he doing? And who was he trying to kid? If he wanted her to stay, if he wanted her to know him, truly know him, and to understand him, then he'd better start relying on trust and faith. As he looked up at her hopeful, beautiful face, and saw the awe and pain in her searching eyes, he acknowledged that he'd also have to rely on his own heart's yearnings, and The Good Lord's promise of hope and redemption.

"I think you know the answer to that question," he told her. "Earlier, when I thought you might be going—I've never felt such panic.''

Reaching up to her, he sat up and took her back in his arms. "You know, last night I found my father's Bible in Eli's office." He took a breath, then told her what was in his heart. "I read some of the passages someone had marked—my mother probably, maybe even Eli, and…it helped me, Issy." He tightened his arms around her, urging her head to rest against the crook of his arm. "There was this one passage about the value of friends. It said, 'Two are better than one.' It said that when one falls alone, he doesn't have anyone to lift him up."

Isabel shifted in his arms, and he wondered if she felt the urgency of his grip, the beating of his heart like a trapped bird trying to escape its cage.

"Tell me, Dillon."

Dillon swallowed, touched his lips to her hair, then continued. "I was so alone after I left Wildwood. So alone. And when I fell, I fell hard and fast. I…I didn't have anyone there to lift me up."

Isabel remained still, but he could see the tears glistening in her eyes when she looked up at him. "Dillon," she said, his name muffled as he held her close. "Dillon—"

His sigh was filled with a deep trembling. "I *do* need you, Issy. I need you to be here in case I fall again. You always were the best friend I ever had, and that verse from Ecclesiastes is very true. Two are better than one."

Isabel lifted her face then, the tears glistening and wet on her cheeks. He'd just told her he needed her, as a friend if nothing else. And oh, how he'd struggled with the telling. She could see it in his face, the pain, the pride, the weariness of someone who'd traveled a long road to find his way home again. And she also saw the longing to be held, just held, unconditionally. How many times had she felt that same longing in her own heart?

"I'll stay, Dillon," she said, tears making her

words shaky and broken. "I offered you my help once, remember? And I meant that with all my heart. We'll fight this, together."

He closed his eyes, then lifted his head up to the sun. "And will you be there when I fall?"

"You won't fall," she whispered. "But I promise, I'll be there, good or bad, to lift you up. You won't have to go through this alone."

Then she pulled his head back down to hers and sealed the deal with a kiss. For these few precious minutes, at least, Dillon could forget all about Eli and his problems. For now, just being here amid the wildflowers with Isabel in his arms was enough. And all the more proof for him to believe God had sent him home for a reason.

Tomorrow, they'd find a way to save the very land that had abided and held them together like a threefold cord all these years.

Gaining strength from Isabel's trust and willingness to help him, Dillon remembered another verse from Ecclesiastes. "A threefold cord is not quickly broken."

Chapter Thirteen

Isabel snapped another picture of the figure sitting on the floor in the middle of the empty room. With the early morning light pouring in from a nearby window, Dillon looked as natural and content as a man could look surrounded by open textbooks and crumpled farm manuals. Except when the camera caught his gaze. The turmoil and determination raging against each other in the depths of his eyes told the tale of the past few days. This was no common man; he wouldn't quit until he had this all sorted out and found a way to help his brother and save this land.

Watching him, Isabel knew she'd made the right decision by staying here with him. When Dillon looked up from studying the latest crop report, his eyes held hers in such an intimate gaze, she couldn't deny that she was glad for any excuse to be with him.

"You're frowning," he remarked as he dropped the folder and leaned back against the wall. "I thought that was my job."

"Just thinking," she told him. Placing her camera on the planked floor, she strolled across the empty parlor, enjoying the morning breeze that teased at the thrown-open floor-to-ceiling windows. Tugging at her haphazard ponytail, she focused on a peeling spot of rose-patterned wallpaper. "What else can I do to help?"

Dillon stretched his legs out, then crossed his booted feet at the ankles, his deceptively lazy gaze moving over her face. "You've already done more than enough. You didn't desert me." Then he asked, "How are things on your end?"

Memories of his words to her just yesterday washed over Isabel, making her flush with joy and hope. Attempting to waylay her optimistic feelings, she slid her hands in the back pockets of her jeans and said, "Well, I have to find out about possible places for my grandmother to move. So far, those places have been slim to none, unless we consider putting her into a nursing home in Valdosta or Albany."

"Not an option," Dillon said as he reached out a hand to her. "Martha is not nursing home material. Do you know your grandmother gets up at dawn every day to take a long walk?"

"She is pretty amazing." Laughing to hide her own fears, Isabel lifted a hand to accept the one he offered her, then settled down on the hardwood floor next to Dillon. Scanning the array of research books and disorganized files, she said, "I think you've checked out every book in the Wildwood library."

"Trying to get a handle on land management and cotton farming, sugar."

Isabel knew he already had a handle on the situation. He'd stayed up most of last night, going back over the records, calling bankers in the middle of the wee hours, talking with the family lawyer. Then, early this morning, he'd organized the workers, giving them irrigation, pesticide, and herbicide schedules to try to salvage the cotton crop. But basically, he was spinning his wheels. Short of a windfall, part of his heritage would still be going up on the auction block come Saturday.

"Do you think you can save this place?" she asked, her fingers still laced with his.

Dillon lifted his head, his gaze roaming around the big, empty room. In typical Dillon style, he ignored her question, choosing instead to admire his surroundings. "Look at these ceilings, will you? So grand and lofty. That ceiling medallion around the chandelier was hand-carved."

Isabel tilted her head to study the yellowed, rose-etched wooden pattern that formed a beautiful, ornate raised circle in the center of the ceiling. "How could Eli let something like this happen?" she wondered out loud.

Dillon dropped her hand then. Jabbing a fist against one of the crop manuals, he said, "I'll tell you how. It's like you said—greed and mismanagement. He overextended himself before he got a good handle on growing cotton. It's like he got the cart before the horse. He went out and bought all the right equipment, hired the best workers, built himself a fancy new house and a nice storage barn, then threw a few thousand cotton seeds in the ground and waited for them to bring him a profit."

"Will they?" she asked, her gaze drifting to the budding cotton bolls out in the distant fields. In spite of the heat outside, the sight looked like snowflakes against a blanket of green.

Dillon let out a huff of a breath. "It would be something. From everything I've found out from talking to the few remaining workers and studying his crop reports, he's done it all wrong. He's overfertilized, thinking to cause a growing spurt, he's overwatered way too early, which could bring on a fungus and possible boll rot, and in spite of the boll weevil eradication program, he's got some pest problems because he can't keep track of his herbicide schedule. It's all been hit-and-miss at best."

"And I always thought Eli was the farmer in the family," Isabel said, surprised.

Dillon looked away, as if he didn't want to continue this conversation. "He always tried to be. He wanted to be the best in order to please our father."

"But?"

He shook his head. "Don't make me talk about this, Isabel."

"I stayed to help you, remember?" She nudged at his muscular forearm. "Tell me, Dillon."

He sighed, then plunged ahead. "Most people around here don't realize this, but Eli never was very smart in school."

"Really? *I* certainly never knew that."

"Another Murdock secret. He always had trouble figuring things through. You know he waited a few years before he went to college, then when he was in college and I was in my first year of high school, I used to help him with his homework."

Amazed, Isabel shook her head. "I would have thought it was the other way around."

"Most people did. I mean, I was the wild child while he walked the straight and narrow. But he struggled all through school, only my mother's support and her hardheaded bullying of his teachers saved him. When I was old enough to understand, I helped him and covered for him. He got into college strictly on our father's name, and he came home on weekends so we could have study sessions together, but then after I left town...well, he never finished. He really wanted a degree in agriculture, to validate his dedication to being a farmer."

"I always wondered why he dropped out," Isabel said, remembering all the rumors she'd heard about Eli wanting to quit college to help his father run the plantation, the way he'd done right out of high school. "Everyone thought he was being noble—you know, taking some of the load off your father."

Dillon picked up a piece of paper he'd scribbled some notes on, then crushed it in his hands. Throwing the discarded wad across the room, he said, "Yeah, he was being noble all right, while I was out gallivanting and sewing my wild oats."

Noting the bitterness of his admission, Isabel touched a hand to his arm. "You still blame yourself for this, don't you?"

He didn't answer right away, but the guilty look he shot her told her she'd hit right on the mark. "If I'd stayed here to help him out, if I'd come home after our father died, things might be different now."

"You don't know that, Dillon."

"I abandoned him, Isabel. No wonder this place is in such an uproar."

"And look how he's always treated you," she reminded him. "He used to bully you and tell you you were worthless, or have you forgotten that?"

"I haven't forgotten anything," Dillon retorted hotly. "But he did always manage to bail me out of the tough spots, too. Can't you see, Eli wanted to make me look small and unworthy because that's the way our father made him feel all the time. And he came to my rescue just so he could rub my nose in it."

"What do you mean?"

Pulling his knees up, Dillon propped his elbows on his denim-clad legs. "Our father would tease Eli about his bad grades. He'd call him stupid and tell him he'd never amount to anything."

She shook her head. "I'm still amazed that this was happening and nobody knew. Your father always seemed so pleased with both of you. He'd brag and go on about his two handsome, smart sons, and now you're saying it was all a sham."

"I know it's hard to believe," Dillon agreed. "But that was just part of the punishment, almost like a cruel reminder to us of what we really were. In private, things would always turn nasty. If he wasn't badmouthing Eli, he'd turn to me and point out what a no-account I was. He told me over and over again how disappointed he was in me and that I'd better shape up, or he'd boot me out the door." He let out an irritated sigh. "Then, of course, he'd find a shred of conscience and forgive me of my transgressions. So that became the pattern. He wasn't so forgiving of

Eli, which is why Eli tried so hard to win his favor. Because of that, Eli also grew to resent me.''

Stunned, Isabel shifted and crossed her long legs. ''So Eli stopped defending you, and you turned against each other?''

Dillon glanced up then, the shame evident in his dark gaze. ''Yeah, then it became sort of a game to see which one of us could win Daddy's favor. Our father pitted us against one another. He'd get Eli going on my bad attributes, then step back to watch the fireworks. Sometimes, they'd gang up on me. Eli would have done anything to win my father's approval.''

Horrified, Isabel said, ''And your mother just turned a blind eye to all this?''

He looked out the window, as if remembering. ''She'd be in the kitchen, humming, or out at some country club function. And even if she had wanted to say something, she didn't dare try to defy my father. You have to remember, my mother comes from the old school that teaches women to stay in their place.''

Reaching out a hand, Isabel caught his hand in hers. ''All those days we ran around this place together, and I never knew. You never once told me.''

Dillon looked up to the ceiling, then pulled his hand away. In one fluid movement, he was up and stalking across the aged floor. ''This is why I don't like to talk about my past. I can't stand that pity I see in your eyes.''

Isabel hopped up to confront him. ''Pity? Is that what you think, that I pity you?''

He whirled, his eyes a dark, raging storm. ''Well, don't you?''

Aggravated, Isabel tossed a hand in the air. "I guess I feel some pity, only because it sounds as if you went through a horrible time back then," she admitted, "but mostly, I feel…I feel so proud of you, Dillon."

Clearly confounded, he put his hands in his pockets and rocked back on the scuffed heels of his boots. "How can you be proud of me after what I just told you?"

She came to stand by him, then touched his arm. "Because if I remember correctly, you never once inflicted that same kind of torment and pain on your brother. Sure, you and Eli fought all the time, but that was mostly because you felt you had to defend yourself, and you defended me a lot, too, back then. Dillon, you kept Eli's learning disability a secret, in spite of everything. All this time, you've protected your brother. Why would you do that, after what he put you through?"

Dillon looked down at her then, his eyes a misty pool of longing and tenderness. "That's simple, Issy. I love him."

Several hours later, Isabel strolled back up the wildflower path. She'd spent the entire day helping Dillon go over the records. Together, they'd managed to get them in some semblance of order, for the bankers and lawyers, if for nothing else. Behind her, the sun was hovering over the trees, its vanishing rays giving the entire sky a bluish pink shimmering cast. The weatherman was predicting rain over the next few days, but Isabel couldn't tell it from the brilliance of this sunset.

As she reached the small backyard, she heard someone humming a sweet tune, then recognized it as one of her favorite hymns—"Just A Closer Walk With Thee." Her grandmother, obviously. Walking around the house, Isabel spotted Martha sitting on a gardening stool in the middle of her prize tomatoes, cucumbers, and purple-hull peas.

Isabel's heart filled with an abundant love as she stood by the back steps, watching her grandmother lovingly tend to her small garden. Martha wore an old, men's work shirt and an Atlanta Braves baseball cap. She seemed perfectly content, as if she didn't have a care in the world.

Swallowing heavily, Isabel once again wondered how Eli Murdock could have let this happen. True, they'd never owned this land or this house but it was home. Well, this old rickety house might not belong to her, Isabel thought, but suddenly it seemed very precious to her, and worth any fight. And it had taken her too long to see that she'd had a good, stable home here, with loving parents who only wanted the best for her. Dillon had been right. Compared to his dysfunctional family, Isabel had had the things that really mattered, but had wished for all the things that really didn't count for much now.

Placing her camera equipment on the steps, she hurried over to her grandmother. "How's it going?"

Martha glanced up, squinting underneath the blue of her hat. "Hi, sweetie. Did you and Dillon get anything accomplished today?"

Falling down on her knees in the soft carpet of loam, Isabel automatically started pulling random weeds away from the tender tomato stalks. "Not much, I'm afraid. But he assures me he's got a Plan B in the back of his mind. By the way, thanks for bringing over those sandwiches.''

Martha gave her a playful wink. ''No problem. I walked over to see Cynthia and took her some apple cake. She's in a bad way. She's so distraught, she's canceling all her commitments and she's hardly answering the phone. This has completely thrown her out of kilter.''

''I can certainly understand that,'' Isabel replied as she sat back to stare off in the distance. ''How can *you* keep a smile on your face, Grammy? How can you sit here in your garden, humming a happy spiritual, when our whole world seems to be falling apart?''

Martha stopped her digging, then carefully put down her mud-caked spade. Turning to give her granddaughter a serene look, she said, ''Why, Isabel Landry, how can *you* ask me such questions?''

Isabel saw that spark of indignation in her grandmother's warm eyes. ''Well, look around,'' she said, swinging her arms wide. ''We could lose all this. I'm worried sick, Grammy, and I don't know what to do about it.''

''So you think I should just give up and mope around, wringing my hands in helpless frustration?''

Isabel tried to picture that particular image, then seeing the traces of amused indignity in her grandmother's eyes, managed to smile herself. ''Well, no, I've never seen you wringing your hands in any sort of frustration.''

''Nor will you ever,'' Martha replied with a

chuckle. "Child, I have complete faith in God's plan for me."

Isabel nodded. "Okay, I can buy that, but what if God's plan involves you having to find a new place to live?"

"Then I'll start looking."

"How can you be so calm about this?" Isabel questioned. "There aren't many available places to rent around here."

"I'll find something," Martha assured her as she turned back to her digging.

"The Lord will provide?"

"Yes, but The Good Lord also gave me a brain and enough sense to start looking in the classified section for rental property."

"And what if you don't find any?"

"I'll cross that bridge when I come to it."

"You amaze me," Isabel stated, shaking her head.

Martha looked back over at her. "Isabel, darling, I've lived on this earth a long time. And I've learned to take the bad with the good. I've buried your grandfather and both your parents, so I've known grief and despair, but I have also known happiness and joy. And I've learned to roll with the punches." Raising a hand to ward off any protests Isabel might voice, she added, "When your grandfather passed away all those years ago, I moved in here with you and your parents, remember?"

"Of course," Isabel said, smiling in spite of her worries. "I missed Grandpa, but I was happy you came to live with us."

"Yes, it turned out okay," Martha continued. "I was so afraid I'd be in the way, a burden on all of you. But your father and mother took me into their home with open arms. In the end, it worked out for the best because I had to take care of them—and you."

"You sure did," Isabel said, her voice quieting. "And you've also done your share of work for the Murdocks." Pointing toward the house, she added, "Look at this place—paint peeling, porches leaning. Never once have they offered to fix things around here, and now, we're losing what little we have left."

Martha finished her work, then took off her thick cotton gloves. Gathering her basket and spades, she sat back on her stool. "Eli isn't doing this to get revenge on us, Isabel. He's become a very desperate man. He has no choice."

"Hmmm. So desperate he waited until he was away on his honeymoon to spring this on everyone."

"He's ashamed and he's hurting," Martha told her. "And we need to pray for him."

Isabel jumped up. "I have prayed for Eli Murdock. But it's hard praying for someone who's only brought me misery."

Martha placed her hands on her hips. "Isn't that just a tad like the pot calling the kettle black?"

"What's that supposed to mean?"

"You're sure ready to forgive Dillon his past transgressions, but not his brother?"

Tugging at a particularly stubborn root of Johnson grass, Isabel said, "I love Dillon, and I know in my heart he's changed. He came back here to make amends, but Eli has pushed him away at every turn."

"Ah, but did Dillon ever once tell his brother how he felt?"

"No, of course he didn't. He was too...too ashamed."

Suddenly realizing she'd been backed into a corner of her own making, Isabel bit her lip, then rolled her eyes. "Okay, okay. Point taken. Dillon was too ashamed to approach Eli, and Eli was too ashamed to tell anyone he was about to lose Wildwood." Sitting back down, she gave her shrewd grandmother a small grin. "What is it with men and their stubborn pride, anyway? I guess they're both pretty hardheaded, aren't they?"

"Yes. And, they *both* need our prayers."

Reaching out to take her grandmother's hand, Isabel gave Martha a quick kiss on the cheek. "But how can *you* not be worried, Grammy?"

Martha patted Isabel's hand. "Psalm 46 tells me not to worry—'God is our refuge and strength, a very present help in trouble.'"

"Will God provide you with shelter?" Isabel had to ask.

Martha nodded. "Yes, if I'm smart enough to seek that shelter myself. Remember, the Bible says that in my father's house are many mansions. I guess it depends on how you look at things—some want a mansion here on earth, some just want the peace of knowing their soul is secure."

Isabel wanted that peace herself. "Your soul is secure, isn't it, Grammy?"

"I'm working toward it," Martha said. "Child, would you look at that glorious sunset." She reached out her wrinkled hand, as if to touch the very rays of the fading sun. "That right there is enough to make anyone feel secure."

Seeing the dancing sun and lace-edged clouds made Isabel suddenly miss watching the sun set over the Atlantic Ocean up in Savannah.

"My offer still stands. You could come and live with me in Savannah."

Martha chuckled. "And all those characters you allow to sublet your apartment?"

"I'll just explain to them that I have a new roommate—or better yet, I'll find a new apartment, or maybe even a small house. You could go to the beach every day, if you wanted, and grow a garden. And you'd love Savannah. You could explore the old city to your heart's content and join the historical society. Lots to do there."

Martha stood up then, and Isabel followed suit. "Wouldn't you like that, Grammy?"

Tears formed in the depths of Martha's eyes. "I'd love that, honey. And we'll see if it has to come to that."

"I feel better now," Isabel said as, arm in arm, they strolled toward the house.

"I told you the Lord would give us the answer," Martha reminded her.

"Does that mean you're ready to go with me? We could leave whenever you say."

"What about your grand plan to help Dillon?"

"I mean, after we get this auction thing resolved."

"And where exactly will that leave things between the two of you—after you've fought the good fight?"

Isabel stopped to stare down at her grandmother's questioning face. "I don't know. I honestly don't know."

"C'mon in, honey," Martha said, tugging Isabel

up the steps. "I've got corn bread and a chicken pot-pie in the oven."

"Umm, sounds great."

Martha faced her before opening the screen door. "It will all work out, Isabel. You and Dillon have a special bond, and...the Lord has plans for you two."

"I'll keep that in mind," Isabel replied sagely.

When the sounds of wheels scraping across the rocks lining Eli's long drive caught their attention, Isabel craned her neck to see who was visiting Cynthia. Then her heart literally dropped to her toes.

Grabbing her grandmother's retreating shirttails, she said, "Grammy, look!"

"What on earth?" Martha came back out to the end of the porch, her eyes going wide as she glanced over at Isabel. "Well, I declare—"

"It's Eli and Susan," Isabel said, her hand flying to her heart. "They weren't scheduled home until Friday. I guess Susan's honeymoon got cut a little short."

Chapter Fourteen

Dillon heard his brother's car turn into the gravel driveway across the stretch of country road. So, Eli had come home early. That either meant he was worried about what he'd done, or he'd found out Dillon was still here. Wanting to get this over with, Dillon stomped across the wide porch and down the cracked steps, headed for a confrontation that had been a long time coming.

Just help me, Lord. Just give me the strength to face him without hurting him. Give me the courage to admit I was a part of all of this, the courage to help him.

Not bothering to knock, Dillon entered the back door of Eli's house, willing himself to stay calm. He had a lot riding on this, but he meant to end it here tonight, one way or another.

Eli was standing in the kitchen, with Susan on one side and Cynthia on the other. The tension in the room hit Dillon squarely in the face as the three of them turned to see who'd just rammed through the door. Susan had obviously been crying. The new bride looked tired and drained. And his mother looked old, her usually impeccable clothes now wrinkled and haphazard, her eyes red-rimmed and devoid of the heavy makeup she normally wore.

But it was the look on his brother's face that stopped Dillon in his tracks. Eli's expression ranged between despair and rage. He looked as if he'd aged overnight. Which suited Dillon just fine, since he felt the same way.

"Well, hello all," Dillon said as he closed the door with a bang. As he faced his brother, all charitable thoughts flew by the wayside. "Home so soon, brother? What's the matter, your conscience get the better of you?"

"Just shut up," Eli warned with a wagging finger. "I'm home because our poor mother called me in a crying fit, telling me you were going through all my files and records. What gives you the right to come into my home and rifle through my private documents?"

Dillon edged close, his hands on his hips, his expression grim. "I'll tell you what gives me the right— my name. I'm still a Murdock, and you should have discussed this financial problem with me, since I still have *the right* to know what goes on on this land."

Eli glared over at him. "You gave up your rights when you left here, brother."

"Maybe so, but I'm back now and I intend to stop this sale."

"How?" Eli asked, his dark eyes blazing with a dare, and maybe a little hope.

Seeing the genuine worry in his brother's eyes, Dillon took a long breath and silently asked God to help both of them. "I haven't figured out how yet, but...Eli, I'm willing to mortgage my business if I have to, to get the money to save this place."

"I don't want your money," Eli said. "You'll never have enough money to pay back what you owe, brother."

Susan began to cry again, softly at first, then in sobs that shook her entire body. Cynthia came around to take the woman in her arms, talking to her new daughter-in-law in hushed, fretful tones.

"See what you've caused with your meddling?" Eli said, waving a hand toward the two women. "Susi and I were supposed to be on our honeymoon, but you've managed to ruin that for us, too."

Indignation coloring his words, Dillon groaned. "You can't be serious? How could you even go on a honeymoon, knowing that you were about to lose part of our land? Did you really think you could let this happen simply by waiting until after the wedding? Did you think I'd leave, and that I'd never find out about this taking place?"

Eli's haggard expression filled with hurt. "Leland told me he'd wait a few days. And I didn't think you cared anymore, little brother."

"Why didn't you tell me, Eli?" Dillon said, his tone soft now. "I could have tried to help."

"Oh, sure. I relied on your help for a long, long time, but you left and I learned to do things on my own. I don't need your help now. I'm doing what has to be done. And there is no way you can stop it."

"Well, don't be so sure," Dillon warned. "I've got

my lawyers working on this, and I can promise you—
I will do whatever it takes to end this thing. I can't
let our home slip away, Eli.''

"What home?" Eli said, bitterness cracking his
voice. "Why should I care? That house means nothing to me. I built my own house." Glancing over at
Susan, he added, "And I intend to raise my children
here—not over there in that run-down white ele-
phant." He hung his head. "I didn't know it would
come to this, though."

For the first time, Dillon saw the torment in his
brother's eyes. He'd never considered that Eli held
only bad memories of their childhood home.

"I can understand your wanting your own life,
your own home, Eli," he said now, "but you went
about it all wrong. If we can sit down and talk about
this—"

Susan interjected then, her blue eyes wide and
misty. "I tried to tell Isabel. I tried to tell her that
you needed to know about this."

Dillon's heart lurched as her words hit him in the
gut like pointed arrows. He must have heard her
wrong. "What did you say?"

Susan wiped her eyes and lifted her chin. "I said,
Isabel knew about this. She's known for days now.
She didn't know about the auction—nobody but Eli
knew about that. But she did know things were bad
financially around here. I told her all about it before
the wedding."

Cynthia gave her daughter-in-law a harsh look.
"Susan, you shouldn't have gone around discussing
this with other people."

Flipping her blond curls, Susan said, "I only told

Isabel that Eli was in financial trouble, and that he was so worried I was afraid we might have to change our wedding plans.'' Looking frantic, she hastily added, ''Well, I had to tell someone! I wanted her to talk to Dillon and see if he'd help out.''

Both Eli and Dillon stared over at her, but Eli spoke first, his tone full of disbelief and anger. ''You discussed my private affairs with that…that trash?''

Without thinking, Dillon bolted across the room, grabbing his brother by the collar. ''Don't you ever call Isabel that again, do you hear me? Isabel wouldn't do something like this—that's more your style.''

Trying to pull them apart, Susan shouted, ''Well, it's true. She knew this might happen, but she was afraid to discuss it with you, Dillon. If you don't believe me, talk to her yourself!''

''I will.'' Letting Eli go, he turned to the cordless phone sitting on the counter.

''Don't you call that woman over here,'' Eli warned. ''She doesn't have any business getting in the middle of our affairs.''

''Her grandmother could soon be out on the street,'' Dillon reminded him, his fingers jabbing the numbers. ''I think that makes it her business.''

Turning away from the scorn in his brother's eyes, he thought back over the last few days, a sick kind of dread pooling like a liquid heat in the bottom of his stomach. Had Isabel known all along? Then he remembered little fragments of conversation. *Eli could use a brother right now. Eli could use your help.* Had she tried to warn him?

Her voice, sweet and warm, came across the line, breaking into his thoughts. "Hello?"

Swallowing back disappointment, Dillon said, "Isabel, it's me. I'm at Eli's house. Could you and your grandmother come over here. We need to talk."

Eli broke the unbearable silence while they waited for Isabel and Martha to arrive. "I told you that girl was trouble—she always has been." With a smug shrug, he added, "I wonder why she didn't bother telling you—I would have thought she'd take pleasure in seeing me suffer."

"Maybe you misjudged her," Dillon retorted.

"I doubt it," Eli replied, but his gaze was wary. "She probably just decided none of this was worth her precious time. She's never cared about this land, but she's sure always wanted to get her hooks in you."

Dillon jabbed a finger in the air. "I told you to quit talking about Isabel that way."

"Still sweet on her, huh?" Eli teased. "Guess some people never learn."

"You certainly haven't," Dillon replied, the last shreds of his patience snapping. "We're all in this mess because *you* didn't tell any of us that the bank was taking over Wildwood."

"Isabel could have warned you," Susan repeated, her own smug look telling him that she would be loyal to her husband, friendship aside. "Apparently she didn't think it was important enough to bother you with, though."

Amazed, Dillon said, "Oh, so now it's convenient

to put all of the blame for this on Isabel? Why didn't either of you see fit to clue me in on this situation?''

"Because there's nothing you can do," Eli said.

"And because you've never cared what happens here," Susan added hotly.

Dillon shook his head. "You two were made for each other."

"Hey, watch it," Eli replied. "You'll show my wife the proper respect."

Dillon huffed a breath. "Oh, that's rich, coming from someone who's never shown the Landrys or anybody else in this town any respect."

"Don't start again," Cynthia said, the tone in her voice brooking no argument. "I mean it, boys. I won't have you two fighting over that girl again."

Curious, Susan whirled to glare at her husband. "What does she mean? Have you fought with him about Isabel before?"

"It was a long time ago, honey," Eli said, his hand touching her shoulder. "Nothing for you to worry about."

Susan crossed her arms over her chest. "You could have told me about it."

"We'll discuss it later," Eli said, his tone firm. "Right now, I've got more important things on my mind—like why you had to go and drag that woman into our business."

A knock at the door brought Susan's head up. Dillon didn't miss the streak of self-righteousness in her eyes. She had told him this deliberately, to take the heat off her husband.

Cynthia opened the door. "Please come in."

Isabel ushered her grandmother into the room, her

eyes moving from Dillon's stony face to Eli and Susan. Susan shot her a knowing look, then held fast to her husband's arm.

"What did you need to talk to us about, Dillon?" she asked, hoping they couldn't hear the tremble in her voice.

Before Dillon could respond, Eli spoke up. "Susan told us she shared some of my private concerns with you—without my knowledge—before the wedding. Seems she wanted you to talk to my little brother about my problems." His expression pleased as punch, he added, "But for whatever reasons, you didn't tell him anything and now...well, he's gone and got his feelings hurt."

"Shut up," Dillon warned his brother, his head down, his fists clenched against the counter.

Martha gave Eli a harsh look, then turned to Isabel. "What's he trying to say?"

Dillon looked up then, his face full of torment. "Yes, what is he trying to say, Issy?"

Isabel's gaze shifted from Eli's condemning expression to Dillon's demanding one. Feeling weak, she leaned against the same counter Dillon was holding on to. "It's true. Susan told me the night of the rehearsal supper that Eli was in some sort of financial trouble."

"And why didn't you tell me about this?" Dillon asked, shaking his head. "You've had plenty of opportunities."

Before Isabel could respond, Eli interrupted, "Because she's a conniving—"

"I told you to shut up," Dillon said, whirling to

glare at his brother. Spiking fingers through his hair, he faced Isabel again, silent and waiting.

Isabel swallowed back her own sorrow and humiliation. Seeing the disappointment in Dillon's eyes caused her heart to tighten inside her chest. She could take anything, but that look. "I didn't tell you... because I wasn't sure if it was my place—"

"You've got that right," Eli shouted. "You don't need to meddle in our business. You don't have any say-so here, little lady."

"I know that," Isabel countered, her indignant gaze never wavering. "You've always made very sure I knew exactly where I stood as far as Wildwood goes."

"Yeah," Eli continued, anger fueling his tongue, "and I saved my brother from making a big mistake. I told him all those years ago, that you were just out to move from the rental house to the big house. You wanted in on a piece of the pie, didn't you, *Issy?*"

"What on earth are you implying?" Martha said, her voice lifting out over the suddenly quiet room. "We've lived on this land for decades now, and we've never once asked for anything from you."

Pointing a finger at Isabel, Eli said, "She wanted more, though. She wanted Dillon. But me and Daddy, we nipped that little fling right in the bud."

Her eyes flying to Dillon's face, Isabel felt the heat of embarrassment rushing across her skin. Dillon looked up, his expression full of apology and...regret.

Humiliated, Isabel asked, "Is there something I should know? What happened back then, Dillon?"

"Yeah, why don't you tell her what happened the day you left Wildwood, little brother?" Eli's expres-

sion was dark and grim. "Tell her, then maybe she'll
have the good sense to leave again. And this time, as
far as I'm concerned, she can take you with her. I'm
not happy about this auction; I tried to stop Leland
from taking our land, but if this will get both of you
out of my life, then I say let him have it."

Slamming a fist down on the counter, Dillon caused
his mother to gasp as pots and pans rattled. "We're
not talking about me or why I left, Eli. I'm trying to
understand why Isabel—or any of the rest of you—
didn't warn me about this auction."

"I didn't know about the auction," Isabel said in
her own defense. "I only knew Eli was in trouble.
And I *did* try to bring it up, several times. But we
had to get through the wedding, and then when I came
to the house on Sunday—"

"She didn't care either way," Susan said now, her
eyes wide. "She didn't tell you, Dillon, because she
was afraid it would distract you—take you away from
her."

"That's not true," Isabel said, appalled that Susan
could turn the tables on her. "Susan, you know that's
not how I felt—I was trying to spare Dillon another
fight with his brother. I honestly didn't know what to
do."

Susan had the good grace to look sheepish, but then
she said, "You told me—you said you didn't want to
get caught in the middle of their problems."

"Yes, but..." Isabel stopped, her head lifting, her
spine straightening. "You know, I don't owe any of
you an explanation for what I did or didn't do. I don't
belong here—I never did. I was perfectly happy with
my life in Savannah, until you called me back."

"My mistake," Susan replied harshly. "If you'll just make sure my wedding pictures are delivered, I'll send you a check in the mail."

"Forget it," Isabel retorted. "You'll get your precious pictures, but I don't want your money."

"That's a hoot," Eli said. "I guess once you found out there might not be any money to be had, you decided to string my innocent little brother along just for fun. Of course, he has managed to eek out a living for himself with those fancy bookstores. Guess you'll have to settle for that."

"Is that really what you think of me?" Isabel said, her voice shaking with rage and sorrow. Turning to Dillon, she repeated her question. "Is that what you believe?"

"Right now, I don't know what to believe," he said on a weary voice. "It would have been nice if someone had warned me about this disaster, though."

The implications of his statement sealed things for Isabel. He would never trust her again; maybe he'd never trusted her at all. And he surely would never be able to love her, not with all of Eli's poison spouting through his mind. Her gaze moved over the worried, defensive faces of the people in the room. There was a quiet desperation here, between these brothers. And it would always be here, holding them at odds. Well, she refused to be a part of it, ever again.

Whirling back to Eli, she told him, "You contradict yourself. First, you tell me I'm just out to get Dillon, then you swear I'm out to get part of Wildwood. What are you so afraid of, Eli, that I'll wind up with both your brother *and* your heritage?"

"I'm not afraid of anything. I'm just protecting what's mine."

Isabel stared at him in awe. "Oh, so that's why you've let Wildwood go into debt?"

"Get out," Eli told her, his finger pointing toward the door. "Get off my land, and take your do-gooder grandmother there with you."

"Eli!" Disgusted, Dillon could only stare at his brother.

Cynthia gasped. "Eli, that kind of talk is uncalled-for. Martha Landry is my friend, and I won't tolerate you being disrespectful to her."

"Sorry," Eli replied, but his expression only grew more harsh. "Mama, there's not much I can do for Miss Martha, anyway. She's gonna have to move once this auction goes through."

Martha spoke up then. "You don't have to tell us twice, Eli. You're a sad, bitter man and you're lashing out, grasping at straws to try to justify your own selfish actions. And right now, you're rejecting the very cornerstone that you need to be holding on to."

"Get out," Eli repeated. "Take your Bible quotes and get out."

"I'm so sorry," Cynthia said, tears streaming down her face. "He doesn't mean it, Martha. You know he doesn't mean it."

"Yes, he does," Martha replied, her own eyes watering up. "But you don't fret for Isabel and me. We'll be just fine."

Dillon had been standing as still as a statue, but now he raised his head. "Isabel, wait."

Isabel turned at the door. "No, Dillon. Eli is right about one thing." Her voice cracked, but she held the tears at bay. "I have always loved you. But tonight, you proved that isn't enough. You can't even trust me enough to tell me what happened so long ago, yet you have the audacity to stand there and judge me simply because I was trying to save you any further pain.

"I waited until after the wedding to talk to you, so I wouldn't be accused of ruining things for Susan and Eli. Then I listened and waited as you told me all your grand plans for Wildwood. I didn't want to be the one to have to tell you the bad news, Dillon. So I waited too long, too late, hoping you'd learn to trust me. And now, I've waited long enough. I'm done with the Murdocks, for good."

Lifting her head, she directed her gaze toward Eli. "Don't worry, we'll be gone by the end of the week, auction or no auction. And as for you two, I hope you don't let this grudge continue to fester. Because if you do, neither one of you will ever be truly happy." Then she looked back at Dillon. "I'm sorry you fought because of me. But whatever caused this rift, whatever part I inadvertently had in it, it stops here and now. I will not be a bone of contention between the two of you. Maybe with me out of the picture again, you can work together to save Wildwood. After all, that is what matters the most to both of you, right?"

Chapter Fifteen

"I didn't think it would matter to me so much, Grammy," Isabel said as they put the last of a set of old, chipped dishes into the large moving box. "I didn't realize how much I loved Wildwood or this old house, until it was too late."

All around them, the house sat still while a soft drizzle covered the surrounding countryside in a fine mist. In every corner, boxes sat marked for either storage or transfer. They'd reached a tentative plan. Martha would move to Savannah with Isabel for the rest of the summer.

As to where her grandmother would live permanently, a small house close to the unincorporated town of Wildwood proper was coming up for sale in the fall, and if Isabel could swing the financing, she intended to buy it for her grandmother. She'd already spoken to the man who owned it. Now, if she could just work out the details.

In the meantime, as Martha had pointed out, they'd

have some time together, then each get back to their own lives. But she refused to live indefinitely with her granddaughter—she thought it best if Isabel and she both continued to maintain their own space and independence.

"Oh, honey," Martha replied now, reaching across the box to give Isabel a hug, "we're going to be all right. We'll survive and we'll just chalk this up to a new adventure, a new path in our faith journey."

Isabel sat back on the footstool she'd pulled up to the deep box. "You amaze me, Grammy. You're dealing with all of this much better than I am."

Martha's soft chuckle filled the still morning. "That's because I don't have a vested interest in this place the way you do."

"You mean Dillon."

Martha nodded. "Still hasn't come around, huh?"

Isabel shook her head, her eyes automatically going to the window, her mind moving toward the looming presence of the house that Dillon had been holed up in since Eli had come home. "I can't blame him. It was wrong of me to keep all of this from him."

Martha took a sip of the hot tea she'd brewed earlier. "Your heart was in the right place. And you were right—you don't need to be at the center of those boys' troubles."

"Which apparently I have always been," Isabel reminded her. "But I guess that doesn't matter any more."

Martha stood up to stretch. "What say we take a little midmorning break? I've got chocolate chip cookies."

"Sounds good," Isabel said, her tone dull and absent. Standing herself, she dropped the stack of *Wildwood Weekly* newspapers she'd been using to wrap plates, then walked over to the open screen door.

The rain colored everything in shades of gray and blue, and gave the old mansion a melancholy look that tore through Isabel's consciousness with such a poignant tugging she had to suck in her breath. Why did this pain feel as if it would literally rip her body in two? Why did loving Dillon so much have to be so wrong?

Needing to feel the wind and water on her hot skin, Isabel grabbed a lightweight white-and-blue-striped rain slicker, then reached for the small, waterproof camera she kept for just such days. "Grammy, I want to get a few shots of the house in the rain. I'll be back in time to finish up these dishes before lunch."

"What about your cookies?" Martha asked from the kitchen.

"I'll eat them on the way."

With that, Isabel grabbed a couple of the fat, brown cookies from the tin her surprised grandmother was holding, and shoved them in the pocket of her slicker.

"All right," Martha said to herself, her eyes wide as she watched Isabel skip down the slippery steps. "Got to get that one last shot—of Dillon Murdock."

Then, smiling softly, she sat down and munched her own cookie, her eyes roaming around the sad remains of her life here on this beautiful piece of God's green earth.

"Help her, Lord," she said now, her eyes closed in a fervent attempt to intervene where her granddaughter's heart was concerned. "Help them both. Show them the life You envision for them, Dear Father. And while You're at it, how about sending a little inspiration my way, too.''

With that, she finished her cookie and tea, then sat back down to wrap up her memories, in shapes of round and square, some soft with age, others as fresh as the new rain falling outside. She'd never been more lonely, but Martha lifted her eyes to the cloudy sky, and smiled in spite of the ache in her heart.

Isabel snapped another round of black-and-whites, her mind centered on her art, her turmoil settling down a bit as she captured the essence of this land and the old, columned mansion. With the drooping wildflowers in front, and the rows of lush cotton growing in back, the house seemed caught in a time warp. Wildwood's history was tumultuous at best, but the house still held a timeless beauty.

Slaves had worked this land at one time, then once the Civil War had ended that horrid practice, share-croppers, both black and white, had taken their place. Her father had come from a long line of sharecrop-pers, and had continued that tradition. And all the while, the aloof, condescending Murdocks had ruled over the land.

Except for Dillon. For some reason, he had broken with tradition. He had rebelled. Why?

Isabel knew part of that answer. Dillon was a sen-sitive, caring man who couldn't tolerate bigotry or prejudice in anyone, including his own family. Cou-ple that with his hunger for knowledge, his need to educate himself and expand his own horizons and vi-sions, and the puzzle pieces started falling into place.

He'd obviously taken a stand against his father and his brother.

But how had she played a part in that?

Why had Dillon and Eli fought over her?

Probably because Dillon flirted with you one time too many and Eli pushed him into a fight about it.

That had to be it. Eli had probably taunted Dillon to no end, and Dillon had finally snapped. But to the point of leaving for good?

So many secrets, so much pain and resentment, shuttered behind the walls of that old, crumbling mansion. Would she ever know the real story?

The house stared back at her, its windows flung open to the rain, its many roofs and eaves dripping with a pretty tinkling melody of water against tin and shingle. The windows might be open to the outside world, but this house held to its secrets like a widow clinging to a faded family portrait.

Stopping at last, she wiped her small camera down on the inside pile lining of her coat, then dropped it into one of the slicker's large, long pockets. Rising up from her crouched position to wipe raindrops away from her brow, she stilled as memories of being here with Dillon fell all around her with the same gentleness as this endless summer rain.

Three days and not a word from him. He had shut down completely, reminding her of the old, brooding Dillon.

Had she hurt him that badly, or was this just an excuse for him to run away again?

She'd thought about confronting him, just having it out with him once and for all, but her pride wouldn't allow that. After all, she'd bared her soul to him, giving him promises as freely as she'd given him kisses. And he'd taken those promises and thrown them back in her face.

And, she reminded herself bitterly, he'd made no promises of his own. He'd asked her to stay, but now he didn't need her or her misguided help. Or her love.

Closing her eyes, Isabel held her head up to the rain and let the tears she'd held back for so long fall freely down her moist cheeks. "Is this my answer then, Lord? Is this the way it has to be?"

How could he live without her? Dillon asked himself as he stood at the huge, open parlor windows, watching Isabel through the sheer ancient curtains. How could he watch her without losing his heart all over again?

How could he forgive her?

Was there really anything to forgive?

He'd thought about her, day and night, since that terrible scene in Eli's kitchen. And he remembered every nuance, every fiber of *her*. He remembered the disbelief and the disappointment on her pretty face when he hadn't leapt to her defense. He remembered the hurt and the shock in her eyes when she'd realized that he and Eli had fought over her long ago. He remembered watching her go, and wanting to pull her back.

But, coward that he was, he hadn't done so. No, instead he'd buried himself in finding a way to stop this land auction, while he'd buried his feelings for Isabel behind a facade as fragile and torn as these decaying, moth-eaten curtains.

C'mon, Dillon, he told himself now, one hand on

the lace and the other on the window frame. *You know she didn't mean to deceive you. You know you told her to stay away. You could have at least listened to her explanation.*

He knew all of that, but still, it hurt. It hurt because he loved her. And, he'd come so close to telling her all his secrets and…he'd come so close to letting her really see inside his soul.

And all that time, she had been aware that something might happen, that Eli was up to something.

Why hadn't she just told him the truth?

And why haven't you just told her the truth? the voice inside his head echoed right back at him.

Because he'd wanted to protect her.

And maybe, blockhead, that's what she was trying to do for you.

What would happen if he did exactly that? he wondered now. What if he just told her the truth, and hoped for the best, on faith alone?

"Two are better than one."

The verse came into his head, reminding him of a need so great, he shook from the force of it. He needed Isabel. He loved Isabel. And he had been fighting for all the wrong reasons.

"For if they fall, one will lift up his companion. But woe to him who is alone when he falls, for he has no one to help him up."

Dropping the curtain, Dillon stepped back into the darkness of the house, then whirled, his boots clicking with purpose against the old hardwood floors. He knew that before Isabel left Wildwood, he owed her the truth, at least.

At last.

* * *

Isabel *felt* him moving toward her before she saw him. Dillon stalked through the wildflowers, his gray eyes centered on her, his whole body tense, his expression unreadable.

Her heart pounded against the warmth of her slicker as she watched him. Devoid of either coat or hat, he kept coming. Apparently, the man had something on his mind.

But she wasn't ready to hear it.

Not willing to bear the brunt of his wrath, Isabel turned back toward the lane leading to her house.

"Isabel, wait!"

She heard him calling, remembered he'd said those exact same words to her the last time she'd seen him. But still she walked toward home, willing herself to be strong.

"Issy, please!"

That stopped her. That note of despair, that hint of regret. That vulnerable quality she'd sensed in him so many times before.

She turned, her eyes touching on his face, her breath leaving her body in a soft sigh of defeat. "What is it, Dillon?"

He met up with her in the middle of the flowers, in the center of the lane where they'd first fallen amid the blossoms all those days ago.

Reaching out to touch her across the short distance, he took a long, shuddering breath. "I...I want to tell you, Issy. I want to tell you everything."

Thinking she'd heard him wrong, Isabel just stood there with her lips parted. Then, coming to her senses, she asked, "But what about...what about me keeping Eli's troubles from you?"

He shrugged, his hand still on her arm. "A minor technicality, all things considered."

Afraid to move, she whispered, "What made you change your mind?"

He moved his hand up the arm of her wet slicker, to coax a tangled mass of damp, heavy curls off her shoulder. "Yours was the lesser of two evils," he explained. "I figured you didn't owe me any explanations, since I had refused to ever give you any."

"So you thought I withheld what I knew deliberately?"

"No, I thought you did it strictly as a self-preservation tactic. And you were wise to stay out of things."

"Why?"

Placing his hands on her shoulders, he held her with an unflinching gaze. "It's a long, ugly story. But I want you to know, before I tell you everything—I love you, Issy."

She gulped, opened her mouth to speak, but he brought a finger up to touch her parted lips. "Just listen, and while you listen, remember that one thing, please?"

"Okay."

He dropped his hands away, and stepped back. "Eli and I were at the pond, fishing with our father. He and Eli were in one of their less charitable moods, so they started teasing me—about you."

At her hiss of breath, he held up a hand. "Just listen."

She nodded silently.

"Eli told my dad that I was hung up on you. Up until then, Dad had been just kinda ribbing me, but all of a sudden he turned nasty.

"Then my father turned to me and told me to drop that notion. He said Murdocks don't mess with girls like Isabel Landry. That I wouldn't want to wind up marrying beneath myself.

"And I asked if he meant we were better than the Landrys.

"Eli chimed in and said we'd always be better than that 'poor trash.' Then he turned to Dad, and grinned. He mentioned your father, how Leonard had had the nerve to want to buy a house in town. It seemed your father wanted to move off Wildwood. Eli couldn't believe that, considering everything we'd done for him."

Isabel interrupted. "What are you telling me? You knew about my father trying to move away?"

"I knew," Dillon replied, the bitterness choking his response. "Eli told me earlier that day, your father had come to speak with him and my father, asking for a loan to buy a house in town. He wanted to buy it for your mother as an anniversary gift, but of course, he didn't have enough money for the down payment."

He couldn't, wouldn't tell her that Eli had taken great pleasure in mimicking her father—his hat in his hand, his head down, his voice shaky.

"I remember when that all occurred," Isabel said, her tone so quiet Dillon could barely hear it above the drizzle. "He was so excited about that house. He told Mother and me it would be a new beginning, that they could at last retire in a home they truly owned."

She shrugged. "Then, he just changed completely. When I mentioned the house again, he told me we wouldn't be moving. And he told me to just forget about it. But I never did."

"Well, neither did I," Dillon replied. "When I asked Eli and Daddy if they'd given the loan to your father, they both laughed in my face.

"Dad said of course he didn't give your father the loan. He figured he'd never get the money back. He didn't feel Leonard Landry had an ounce of backbone. And if he allowed your dad to move into town, he'd start shirking his duties at Wildwood."

Isabel hitched a breath, seeing things in a whole new light. "So my father just gave up, didn't he?"

"He didn't have much choice. He couldn't afford to get fired. And that's exactly what Eli and Daddy threatened to do if he tried to buy that house."

A dark helpless rage coursed through Isabel. "He just wanted something to call his own, Dillon. Something for my mother and me to be proud of. How could anyone be so cruel?"

She hadn't realized she was pounding her fists against Dillon's chest until his hands halted hers.

"I wondered that myself, sweetheart." He swallowed, paused, then said, "And that day, I made the fatal mistake of questioning my father's authority. You see, I defended your father and begged my dad to reconsider. I told him it wasn't right. But he just laughed and said as long as he had people willing to work for room and board and a few acres of crop he'd never give it up.

"I'm telling you, Isabel, it sickened me, watching them make their snide jokes about a man who'd dedicated his life to this place. So I got angry and tried once again to reason with them." He stopped, his eyes lifting to hers. "And that's when Eli started in on you again.

"Eli accused me of wanting to get on your good side. He said I was so busy chasing you around, that I'd forgotten who I was, and who you were. He said low-class girls like you were good for only one thing. Then he made a derogatory remark about you and I lost it. I went after him with both fists."

Humiliation colored Isabel's words. "Oh, Dillon, I'm so sorry."

"Don't be." Lifting a hand to her face, he said, "I told him flat out that I loved you."

Shocked, Isabel raised her head, her gaze holding his. And then, she saw it there in his eyes. Dillon had *always* loved her, even back then.

"You fought against your brother and your father because you *loved* me?"

"Yeah."

"I can't believe you did that, and I never knew."

Dillon lowered his head to briefly touch her forehead. "That's because my father got so mad. He told me that if I ever went near you again, he'd kick your family off this land and he'd make sure your father never found work in the state of Georgia." He swallowed again, then looked away, off in the distance. "Then he told me if I didn't like the way he operated, I should get off Wildwood and never come back. I didn't give him time to take back those words. I knew I had to get away. I had to leave, or I'd become just like them."

Isabel's hands were shaking. Reaching up for him,

she touched her fingers to his face. In a cry filled with anguish, she said, "Are you telling me you left Wildwood to protect my family? To protect me?"

"Yes," he said at last, the one word lifting a tremendous burden off his shoulders. Placing his hands over hers, he moved closer, his gaze holding her. "I loved you, Isabel. And I knew if I stayed here, I wouldn't be able to deny or control that love. So I left."

"I can't believe this," she said, tears falling down her face. "I can't believe a father would do this to a son, or a brother would be so cruel."

"Believe it. But don't feel guilty, honey. Like I told you once before, it had been a long time coming. I'd stood by too many times, watching the sickening way my family dealt with people they considered subordinates. I knew it was wrong, but I never spoke up because of my old need to be loved and accepted. Yet that day I realized I would never be able to stay here. And I knew in my heart that once I took a stand, I'd have a tough battle ahead, and worse, so would you."

"What...what did you do?"

"I walked back home, then I saw you sitting on the old swing that used to be out in your backyard. You had your legs curled up underneath you, and your nose buried in a book." He reached out now to pull at a strand of her soaked curls. "I remember your hair—it was so short and curling all around your head. I wanted to go to you and tell you how I felt, but instead I went to the bank, and with my mother's help, withdrew a large sum of money, and headed north. I enjoyed life to the fullest, soaking all my sorrows in a carefree life-style, partying away my pain, until the money ran out.''

Isabel pulled him close, sorrow evident in her eyes. ''Dillon—''

He hushed her. ''I woke up on a park bench in downtown Atlanta. There was an old man standing over me with a cup of coffee. He owned a bookstore on Peachtree Street, and after I poured out part of my sorry story to him, he hired me—on the condition that I get cleaned up and start going to church.''

''And?''

''And I did exactly that.'' His smile was wry and bittersweet. ''This man saw everything in me that my parents and brother hadn't. He let me read books to my heart's desire, never once calling me a bookworm or a sissy. He let me fiddle with the store, rearranging things to bring in more business. After a year or so, I asked him if I could become his partner. He co-signed a contract that allowed me to buy into the bookstore, and we were in business.'' Dillon's voice became soft then. ''He died five years ago, and his family sold his half of the business to me. I named the chain stores Rhyme and Reason, but that one downtown store will always remain Sweeney's Books.''

''Rhyme and Reason?'' Isabel shook her head, wondering if this man would ever stop surprising her. ''You own Rhyme and Reason and Sweeney's Books?'' Sweeney's was a legendary Atlanta land-mark, and Rhyme and Reason was very popular with book lovers all over the south.

''I own them so far, unless I mortgage the whole lot to save this place,'' he said to her. ''The day I left, I remember my father telling me there was no rhyme or reason to a son turning on his father the way I'd turned on him." He wiped the thickening mist off his forehead. "Well, I found my rhyme and reason."

Isabel started crying all over again. "And you did it because of me—"

"I did it because it was the right thing to do, and yes, because as I told you at the beginning of this sordid tale, I love you. But I was so afraid to tell you that, so afraid you'd be disgusted by what my family had done." He pulled her close. "But I promise you—I'll do whatever it takes to make it up to you and your grandmother. That is, if you'll still have me."

Running her fingers through his wet hair and tugging his head close, she laughed through her tears. "If I'll still have you? Dillon, I love you so much, I'm even willing to stay here at Wildwood and put up with Eli—that's how much I want you."

"We don't have to stay here," he said, hugging her. "I know it's asking a lot—I'm going to do everything I can to save this place, but I need you, Issy. Are you up for the fight?"

"Yes," she told him. "Yes."

He kissed her with a gentle surrender, the last of his defenses shattered by a cloudburst of joy.

Still dazed, still deeply touched by all the sacrifices he'd made for her honor, Isabel pulled back to stare up at him. "I should have told you about Eli's problems, Dillon—"

"It doesn't matter. You couldn't have done anything, anyway." Looking up at the old house, he said,

"Let's face it. The Wildwood we knew is gone. And maybe it's for the best."

When footsteps sounded in the nearby mud, Isabel glanced up to find Susan standing there, tears falling down her face.

"It's not for the best, Dillon," the blonde said as she hiccuped and walked toward them. "You and Isabel love each other, and there's nothing wrong with that. And if you want to help rebuild this place, then I've got some information that will get things started, no matter what my husband thinks."

"What are you talking about?" Dillon asked, his tone wary.

"I'm talking about the deed the lawyers have managed to bury under all those files you've been searching," Susan replied after a loud sniff. "The deed that names *both* of Roy Murdock's sons as co-owners of this entire property."

Isabel's gasp echoed over the wet field. "What?"

"That's right," Susan affirmed, her tone laced with an apology. "Dillon, your name is on the title to this land—your father never did change his will. While I may be stupid in most things, I've heard enough talk between Eli and the lawyers to know that if that's the case—"

"If that's the case, the bank can't auction this land until I have a chance to buy it back!" Dillon said, a new hope rising in his words. "I can stop the auction."

"That is, if you're still interested," Susan said, one hand pushing through her drenched curls. "From the look of things, I'd say you've found what you came back here for—and I don't think it's an old house."

"You're right," Dillon quickly agreed, his hand squeezing Isabel's. "I came back for Isabel—she's more important than Wildwood—"

"But you have to try," Isabel told him. Then she turned to Susan. "Why are you doing this?"

Susan shot her a bittersweet smile. "I've learned a few things over the last few days." She pointed toward the old mansion. "For one—that's the real Wildwood. Eli built himself a showcase, and now he's trapped inside that showcase. When I got home today, I dreaded going inside to face him—he's so bitter and ashamed of what he's done, but he refuses to acknowledge that and take responsibility for his actions. Well, I'm speaking for him." She gave Dillon a pleading look. "He doesn't want to lose this land, but he thinks it's too late."

"We can help him," Dillon told her. "That's all I've ever wanted, for us to be a family again."

Susan nodded, then looked at Isabel. "I'm so sorry. I was wrong the other night, but I was so afraid Eli would hate me. I do love him and after watching you two together today, I can see that you deserve some happiness, too. Eli will spit nails when he hears I told you this, but...somebody had to stop all of this foolishness."

Dillon caught her arm. "He'll forgive you. He loves you." Then he surprised Susan by giving her a brotherly kiss. "Thank you. This means my father forgave me, too."

Susan laughed shakily. "I only hope we *can* forgive each other and find the faith you two seem to possess. I'm going to work on that, too."

"We'll work on Eli together," Isabel said, taking

Susan's hand. Now that she knew Dillon loved her, she could handle his stubborn brother.

"Thank you," Susan replied. With that, she turned to make her way through the mud back to Eli's house.

Isabel watched her go, then turned back to Dillon. "Are you sure we have that faith she's talking about?"

"Very sure. I have complete faith that Wildwood will be restored to its former glory, and I have absolute faith that I'm going to be a happily married man soon."

Isabel thought she couldn't possibly love him any more than she did right this minute. "So you're really going to buy it back from the bank?"

"Oh, I intend to buy it back," Dillon said, "but I don't intend to live in it. I've got a better idea."

"What?"

"You'll just have to wait and see," Dillon replied. "But first, I need to talk to my brother."

"And we probably should get out of the rain. I'm sure I look a mess."

Dillon's eyes filled with love. "No, even soaking wet, you look incredible."

Isabel wrapped her arms around his shoulders. "That's because I've finally found the perfect picture—the one of us together."

"We'll have lots of pictures. First, of our wedding, then our children and grandchildren," Dillon promised as his lips met hers. Raising his head, he said, "I'll always be there to catch you if you fall."

"Two are better than one," Isabel replied.

"Make that three," Dillon said, raising his gaze to the heavens. "A threefold cord is not quickly broken."

Isabel smiled. "Welcome home, prodigal son."

Epilogue

One year later

"Can you believe it's finally happening?"

Isabel turned from the window of the upstairs bedroom to smile at Susan Murdock. "It doesn't seem real, considering I've been in love with Dillon for half of my life, maybe all of my life. But, yes, on a perfect day like today, I can believe it's going to happen."

"You two really fought the odds, didn't you?"

"Yes, but we have more than good odds—we've been blessed, Susan. We all have."

Susan's smile disappeared as she fluffed the skirt of her floral print matron of honor dress. "I just wish Eli would change his mind and come to the wedding. Dillon really wanted him to be his best man."

Isabel looked back out the window, down on the new blooming field of wildflowers where in just a few minutes she would become Mrs. Dillon Murdock. "The day's young, Susan. He might show up yet.

He's come around on Dillon's new crop maintenance plan, and just about everything else we've thrown at him over the past year.''

Susan shook her head. Before she left the room, she said, ''Well, you're getting hitched, with or without my husband's blessings. And…you look so beautiful, Isabel.''

''Thank you.'' Isabel lifted her gaze to her reflection in the beveled mirror. The white linen sleeveless wedding dress was cool and simple, the full skirt falling out around her legs in yards and yards of frothy material that both her grandmother and Cynthia Murdock had worked to create. Her hat was simple, too. White straw with a tiny sprig of wildflowers tucked underneath the linen band. It sat at a jaunty angle over her long, loose curls. Touching a finger to the strand of pearls Dillon had given her, she decided she'd have to do. She didn't want to make a splash as a bride, she just wanted to be with Dillon.

And now that Wildwood was completely renovated and things were back in order, she would have that chance.

True to his word, Dillon had taken most of his savings, investments, and a loan against his business to pay the bank back for the debts owed on Wildwood. Eli had been furious at first, then resigned and humble. Since he no longer owned this part of the land, there was little he could do to protest the proceedings.

Isabel knew he was grateful, though, because he'd forgiven Susan right away. He truly loved his wife, and deep inside, he'd been glad that someone had found a way for him to save face and Wildwood at the same time. And Susan was learning how to handle her husband. She had him attending church each Sunday, granted with a scowl on his face. But Eli was changing. Isabel could tell.

And, this big old house was still in the family.

But it now belonged to the entire community. Dillon had turned the house into a museum. The entire first floor was open to the public each Monday through Saturday.

On the second floor, Cynthia Murdock and Martha Landry now shared twin suites—comfortable, elegant apartments with small kitchens and baths. Together, the two women had formed a partnership—they were the official curators of the Wildwood Foundation.

Martha had agreed to do it only as an *equal* partner. She'd take no more orders from a Murdock. Cynthia had agreed to do it only if both her sons would include her in all of their daily decisions regarding their holdings. She'd not be left in the dark ever again. Both women had been granted their stipulations.

Together, they'd worked to have the mansion registered as a historical landmark. They loved their work, and enjoyed getting paid equally for doing it. Together, they planned teas, showers, weddings and any and every other sort of gathering imaginable on the grounds and in the long, airy dining room located on one entire side of the bottom floor. By giving them this responsibility, Dillon had given them their spirit back. Those two would never be idle in their old age.

Cynthia now kept sharp tabs on both her sons, and kept the lawyers and bankers hopping as she called for updates on the now thriving cotton crop and the Wildwood Foundation.

Both Cynthia and Martha had worked hard to help

Dillon and Isabel renovate the house. While Dillon worked in Atlanta, and Isabel finished up her commitments in Savannah so she could join him there, the two women searched and researched everything it would take to get the house back to its original splendor.

And Isabel's childhood home…well…Isabel smiled and clasped her hands, tears of joy and love brimming over in her eyes. She'd come home one weekend, hoping to meet her future husband here for a few days of painting and scraping, only to find her wedding present waiting for her.

Dillon had completely renovated the shack she'd called home most of her life. It was now an official caretaker's cottage, complete with lacy white shutters and screened porches; white, shining walls and working bathrooms and sturdy floors; and beautiful antique furniture including his great-grandmother's beautiful rice bed which had been removed from the mansion and restored for his bride. No leaky roof, no dips and creaks, no bad memories.

"I told you I'd make it up to you," he'd explained as he'd held her in the cottage's garden. "This is our home, Issy. Yours and mine. We'll always have a place to come back to—we're the official caretakers of Wildwood."

And tonight, she'd be in his arms, there in their little house. Their home.

"Oh, Daddy," she said now as she looked up toward the heavens. "I never understood. I never knew about the sacrifices we have to make for those we love. But you did. And Dillon does, Daddy. He's a lot like you."

Just then a knock at the door brought her head around.

"Coming."

Isabel opened the door to find her grandmother standing before her in a mauve chiffon dress. "It's time, honey."

Grabbing her Bible, Isabel looked around. "Where's my bouquet?"

"Dillon has it."

"That's not traditional—I think I'm supposed to be the one who carries it."

"Dillon's not a traditional sort of man. He picked it fresh—wants to hand you your flowers the minute he sees you."

Touched, Isabel let out a lovesick sigh. "Have you ever known a sweeter, kinder man?"

"Oh, one or two," Martha said, her wink misty.

"Any sign of Eli?"

"No, but the Lord has brought us this far—He won't let us fall now."

They walked down the shining curved staircase, past the dining room where the small wedding cake sat in all of its white-and-yellow splendor, then out onto the front porch. The Wedding March began as Martha escorted her granddaughter down into the garden and onto the open path where the guests were seated just a few feet from the wildflower field. The wildflowers were spread out before Isabel like a wedding quilt, brilliant and dainty, delicate and strong, the perfect decoration for her wedding day.

Dillon stood there, his gray eyes bright with a bursting of emotions, his cream-colored summer suit crisp and dashing, his grin slanted and devastatingly charming. And in his hand, he held a fat bouquet of flowers, freshly picked just for her.

Martha chuckled as she gave Isabel over to him. "She's all yours, son."

"Thank you," he said, his eyes never leaving his bride. "I like the dress, Issy."

Isabel's words held a breathless quality. "You say that about all my dresses."

"But I especially like this one, sweetheart. You are the best-looking bride I've ever seen. And you're mine."

"You've got that right."

The ceremony progressed with the bride and groom completely absorbed in each other. Then the preacher got to the part that asked if anyone objected to this wedding.

"I do," came a bold, deep-throated voice from the back of the rows of white chairs.

A gasp went out over the crowd as Eli hurried up the path, wearing his own white linen suit. "I mean," he said in an even tone, his gaze moving from his wife's frozen expression to his surprised brother, "I object to this wedding taking place without me. I do believe I'm supposed to be the best man."

Dillon closed his eyes, clearly relieved. Then he turned to his brother and reached out a hand. "Thank you, Eli."

Eli accepted the handshake, his eyes brimming with pride and apology. "No, thank you, brother." Then, he began, "Dillon, I—"

"Don't," Dillon said in a soft voice. "We'll talk later, though. We've got a lot of catching up to do."

"Okay," Eli replied, bending his head sheepishly.

Then he turned to the confused preacher. "Well, what are you waiting for? I hear there's going to be a wedding at Wildwood today. Let's get things rolling."

"Amen," Cynthia Murdock said, her wide-brimmed pink hat bobbing in delight. Then she raised her camera and snapped a picture. Looking across at Martha, she wiped her eyes and said, "I just love weddings. Don't you?"

* * * * *

Dear Reader,

I grew up on a farm in south Georgia and lived in a house similar to the one described in Isabel's story. I couldn't wait to leave that house, but it has stayed with me all of these years. My memories are sometimes bittersweet, but I realize now that I loved my home and I often dream of my life there.

The story of the prodigal son has always fascinated me. Coming from a big southern family, I've learned lots of lessons about forgiveness, but this parable teaches all of us that there is sometimes more to the story than what appears on the surface.

In this story, there were two prodigal sons. Dillon lost his way by running away, and Eli lost his way because he'd never learned true humility. Not only does the Bible teach us to forgive those we love, we also have to remember that as human beings, we are all God's children.

I'm glad Isabel and Dillon found each other again, and learned the lessons of forgiveness and acceptance. Hope you enjoyed their story.

Until next time, may the angels watch over you while you sleep.

Lenora Worth

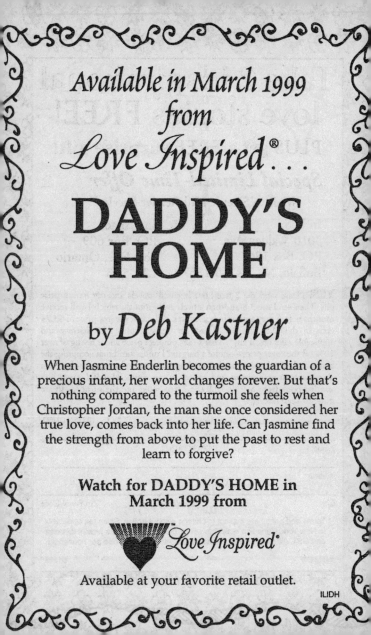

Available in
February 1999
from
Love Inspired®...

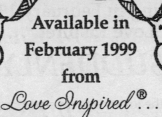

BRIDES AND BLESSINGS

by *Molly Noble Bull*

When Suzann Condry agrees to assume her long-lost twin sister's role as a sweet church librarian, she can't help falling in love with the church's handsome preacher. Will their love survive if she reveals her true identity?

**Watch for BRIDES AND BLESSINGS
in February 1999 from**

Love Inspired®

Available at your favorite retail outlet.

ILIBAB